The Ladies of Harrington House

Spirits of New Orleans

Book Three of the Series

JUDY HORNBECK

A special thank you and much love to my children and their spouses. It is with their generosity that this book is published.

A special thank you to my son for the cover art picture, taken while he stood at Jackson Square. Spirit showed herself just for this book.

TABLE OF CONTENTS

Chapter One	Lenny	1
Chapter Two	Welcome Back, New Orleans	7
Chapter Three	Marie, Charleston	13
Chapter Four	Grace, New Orleans	17
Chapter Five	Marie, Charleston	21
Chapter Six	Cecilia, New Orleans	23
Chapter Seven	Marie, Charleston	27
Chapter Eight	Lenny, New Orleans	33
Chapter Nine	Randy	37
Chapter Ten	Marie	41
Chapter Eleven	Leona, New Orleans	45
Chapter Twelve	Randy	49
Chapter Thirteen	Marie	53
Chapter Fourteen	Randy	57
Chapter Fifteen	Marie	61
Chapter Sixteen	Cecilia	65
Chapter Seventeen	Lenny	67
Chapter Eighteen	Randy	71
Chapter Nineteen	Leona	75
Chapter Twenty	Randy	79
Chapter Twenty-One	Savannah Lamprey's Diary, 1850	87
Chapter Twenty-Two	Randy	133
Chapter Twenty-Three	Marie	137
Chapter Twenty-Four	Lenny	143
Chapter Twenty-Five	Randy	147
Chapter Twenty-Six	Leona	151
Chapter Twenty-Seven	Lenny	157

Chapter Twenty-Eight Marie and Randy 161
Chapter Twenty-Nine Winnie and Lenny 167
Chapter Thirty Randy 173
Chapter Thirty-One Leona and Randy..................... 179
Chapter Thirty-Two A Boat Trip 185
Chapter Thirty-Three Lenny....................................... 191
Chapter Thirty-Four Marie and Randy 195
Chapter Thirty-Five Leona, Charleston 199
Chapter Thirty-Six New Orleans 203
Chapter Thirty-Seven The Family Gathers................ 213
Chapter Thirty-Eight Good-bye and Surprises 219

CHAPTER ONE

Lenny

Leona boarded the airplane for New Orleans late Wednesday afternoon. She was looking forward to seeing her sister, Florence. They both needed a respite from Spirit. Their adventures had led to great friendships and heartaches. I just need rest now, she thought. As she settled into her aisle seat she noticed the nice-looking young man sitting next to the window. His brown hair with shimmers of red was the first thing that caught her attention. There was a soft glow of sunshine that came through the window making it hard to see his face. It was angelic with a hint of darkness.

"Excuse me, ma'am. Would you like the window seat?" He asked politely.

The shadows blocked the sun and she was able to see his face. There was a warmth there behind his eyes and a sadness.

"Thank you, no. I prefer the aisle. I know most people like the window, I don't," Leona replied, "To be honest, I don't like flying.'

Looking at her with a cocked head and concern he said, "It's really very safe. I was a crew chief on a B52 out of Barksdale. I flew everywhere that bird went."

Leona could see that his mind had wandered back to those flights. She realized the young man was trying to make her comfortable, "My name is Leona. I'm heading to New Orleans to meet my sister. Nice to meet you……"

Caught daydreaming, he said, "Oh, sorry. I'm Lenny Renard. New Orleans is home for me," he said looking out the window.

The stewardess announced they had clearance from the tower for take-off, "Please make sure your seat belts are secure and your seats are in an upright position."

Leona tightened her seat belt another notch and took a deep breath. The jet lifted off and once in the air Lenny pushed his seat back a notch and closed his eyes. Leona thought he was right at home in the air. How wonderful to be so trusting. She liked her feet on the ground where she could feel Mother Earth. There was no service on this flight so Leona decided on a short meditation. She closed her eyes, listened to the engines, and called in the Goddesses.

All and all the flight was smooth sailing. As they landed, Leona thanked the Goddess and Mother Earth for the safe flight.

"My sister is meeting me, do you have someone meeting you?" Leona said smiling.

"No, I'm just going to grab a cab. I do this flight often for work," Lenny replied.

"A handsome young man like you doesn't have a wife or girlfriend waiting for you?" Leona laughed. She could see his eyes change for a split second to sadness. Quickly changing the subject she said, "We'd be happy to give you a ride. You did say you were going into the city, correct?"

"Yes, I live just across from the Cafe Du Monde, can you tell by my belly," he said, laughing and patting his stomach.

Leona thought he had the most infectious laugh, there was something very familiar about it. Where had she heard it before?

Laughing with him she said, "My sister lives across the square! You're neighbors."

As the airplane taxied to the gate and stopped, Leona gathered her things. Lenny and Leona made their way to the baggage area where Florence was waiting, waving her arms like a wild woman. There was no way Leona could have missed her dressed like the gypsy she was. Her long jet-black hair still had no gray streaks! Unlike Leona's which was white. And that multicolored long flowing dress with silver bangle bracelets screamed out, 'Look at me,' Leona thought.

She turned to Lenny and said, "Don't be scared, but that's my sister over there," she said, pointing to the wildly waving woman.

"Scared, hell no! She looks like fun to me," he said, laughing as they headed her way.

Introductions were made and Flo was more than happy to take Lenny home. Linking her arm through his, she asked, "So, Lenny, what is it you do for a living?"

"Flo, honestly, if I tell you I have to kill you," he said, looking serious.

Seeing the ladies' reaction he broke out in a hardy laugh. There it was again, Leona thought, I know that laugh.

"Oh, Lenny! You are a card. Why don't you join us for dinner? That's if you're free," Flo said, fluttering her eyelids.

Did she really just flirt with him, heavens, the woman was old enough to be his.....Lenny stopped short. "Flo, are you making a pass at me? Because if you are, I don't think I can keep up with you," he smiled.

The banter between them went on until they got to the car. Lenny threw his bags in the trunk, along with Leona's, then climbed into the back seat.

"I'm all yours, ladies. May I suggest a restaurant?"

"By all means, young man. We are at your disposal," Flo said, winking at Leona.

"It's before you get to the city, right on 61, in Metairie. It's called Queens Cuisine and they have the best soul food around. I figured your creole cooking would be better than any restaurant," he said, tapping Flo's shoulder from the back seat, "So soul food was the next best thing," he said winking at Leona, who had turned to look at him.

"I do believe the boy is trying to get an invite to a home-cooked meal, Flo," Leona laughed.

"Well, you know I like to be neighborly," Flo replied, as she pulled out of the airport parking lot. Dinner was everything he promised. The food was definitely down-home cooking. They told him all about discovering they were sisters and their extended family in Charleston. The food and relaxed conversation went well, right up to Flo's question.

"So, Lenny, tell us about yourself. Married? Girlfriend?"

Lenny put down his fork, wiped his mouth, and signaled the waiter for the check.

"Ladies, this has been nice, but I need to get home. You have been wonderful and I've really enjoyed this," taking the check from the waiter he said, "It's my treat."

The jovial mood was broken. The ladies knew when a Spirit didn't want to be seen and he had one. Gathering their things the group continued their drive into the city. Trying to break the ice again, Leona kept the conversation going with stories about their escapades in Charleston.

As they neared downtown New Orleans Lenny said, "Flo, just park in your area, I can walk across the square. I know how hard it is to park in the city."

Flo pulled the car into an open spot on the street and said, "It was a pleasure meeting you, son. If you need anything, we are just across the square."

"Yes, please, we always welcome company," Leona replied.

"Thank you, ladies, it was a pleasure. I am sure we'll meet again," he said as he got out of the car and grabbed his suitcase.

The ladies watched him walk down the street, "That boy has a dark spirit around him, sad," Leona said.

"I felt it too, it's female. Did you see him change when I asked him if he was married?"

"Yes, but we can't help until he's ready….so sad."

CHAPTER TWO

Welcome Back, New Orleans

It had been a while since Leona had visited New Orleans. Her life was so busy in Charleston the past few years that it made it impossible. With Maggie's and Allison's weddings, Marie's internship, and the birth of the latest family member, Jasmine Grace, things were a bit hectic.

It was her time now. She needed time away from the drama to refresh and clear her chakras. Flo always seemed to know what she needed, not just because they were sisters, but because they were best friends first. It had been a shock when they discovered the long-buried secret of their lineage. Looking back on that time they both agreed they felt the connection before the truth was revealed. Spirit knew the right time for their paths to cross.

The morning sun shone through the window overlooking the river. Leona stood gazing out with intensity as she watched the sparkling fairies dance on the glistening waters of the Mississippi. Fairies always brought good news for Leona. She wondered what these playful Spirits were planning.

"Aunt Leona," Geraldine paused, getting no response, "Aunt Leona," she said louder.

"Oh my, Geraldine! I didn't hear you come in," she said, hugging her niece, "You look great, how have you been?"

"I'm good, how are you?" she said questionably.

"A bit preoccupied I think. It's the fairies, they got my attention," she said nonchalantly.

"Ah, the fairies. It's been a while since I've seen them. We can always use good news I think," Geraldine said, now gazing out at the river.

That was how Florence found them, each deep in their own thoughts, hypnotized by the sparkling waters.

"I see the river has welcomed you back, dear sister."

Turning to face Flo, Leona smiled, "It knows just what I need."

"It's the water, its purity cleanses us. Although it's always moving it remains the same. It's the pulse of life for us," Flo offered as she hugged Leona.

"And so it is…" Geraldine said as she hugged her mother and her aunt.

Geraldine set out the tea and beignets from Cafe Du Monde she had gotten earlier. The ladies sipped and indulged in the warm confectionery sugar-coated pastries. As they did, it reminded them of the young man they had met. Leona told Geraldine the story of meeting Lenny, as Flo just nodded since her mouth was full and covered in white sugar. She told them both that his laugh made a lasting impression, she swore it was familiar.

After finishing their decadent breakfast, Florence and Leona decided on a stroll in Jackson Square. Arm and arm they walked past the Cathedral, past the statue of Andrew

Jackson, and up the stairs to the river. The Steamboat Natchez stood at the pier ahead of them.

"What do you say, sister, are you game?" Flo asked.

"Yes, the river beckons. Lead on!" she laughed.

They paid their fare and made their way up to the rear of the boat. They both loved to watch the huge paddlewheel power through the water. As the boat pulled away from the pier Leona relaxed in the wheel's rhythm. The swish swish swish sound was hypnotic. As they passed the last piling on the dock she heard a familiar laugh. Looking over to the dock she saw Lenny, waving to them.

"Flo, look, it's Lenny. I couldn't forget that laugh," Leona said, yelling above the noise of the wheel. They waved back smiling.

"How the heck could you hear his laugh?

Leona thought for a minute, "I don't know, but I know I heard it. That's why I looked."

"Spirit tells me that we'll meet him again," Flo said.

As the riverboat continued down the river Leona was surprised by the number of industrial areas they went by.

"Where are all the beautiful plantations and huge mansions?"

"Oh Leona, it's not 1850! They just don't exist anymore. We do have a few further up north that have become parks open to the public. This industry," she said, pointing to the shore, "It's what built New Orleans."

They drifted another hour, further down the river until Leona was sure they would reach the Gulf of Mexico.

"I thought by now we would be near the gulf, is it much further?"

"No, we are nowhere near the gulf," Flo replied, "As a matter of fact we are over a hundred miles upstream!"

"No way! Oh my, do I feel stupid? I just assumed it was right on the gulf coast," she said laughing.

"Don't feel bad, most tourists think that," Flo said, as the riverboat made its u-turn to head back to the city.

The ladies enjoyed the remainder of the trip in silence. As they pulled up to the dock Leona looked around for Lenny. He was nowhere around.

Standing on the walkway leading down to Jackson Square Leona said, "This always blows my mind, looking down on New Orleans! The river is actually higher than the city."

"And that's why we are so affected by storms.... remember?" Flo said.

"How could I forget! Katrina, horrible, just horrible!" Leona said, "Grace! We have to see Grace."

Florence explained that she and Grace had kept in touch. Once a month they would meet at The Beignet Cafe for coffee and gossip. It was then that they had decided to plan a late lunch for tomorrow. It would be more like an early dinner since they had to wait for Grace to close her office. 'Mahalia's Place' was thriving and kept Grace busy.

It was the Spirit of Mahalia's house that had brought the women together years ago. Mahalia had died during the storm when her house flooded. She had waited for her granddaughter who never came home. Grace had discovered that she was Mahalia's long-lost granddaughter, Bell, thanks to Flo, Leona, and Maggie. Since then they had all stayed in touch.

After grabbing a quick lunch at the small cafe around the corner from the condo, the ladies headed home. By mid-afternoon, Leona felt the need for a nap. Flo agreed.

"The river breeze and sunshine have plum tuckered me out," Leona said, in her sweetest southern accent laughing.

"I do believe I feel the same way," Flo said, as they both found a comfy recliner to nap on.

Leona faded first, she was in the twilight stage of slumber when she heard her. She tried to wake up but fell deeper into her dream. It was raining, and she couldn't see. There were headlights and suddenly darkness. As the darkness engulfed her she heard a female voice say, ***"You're here to help him."***

She woke up with a start, still feeling the darkness as she went to the window. She stared at the water. Where are you fairies? This dream wasn't good news.

"Leona, are you okay?" Flo said, looking concerned.

"Yes, I just had a dream. It was dark." She went on to explain what she heard and saw.

"He? I wonder who he is? This should be interesting," Flo said.

Leona knew but was afraid to say it out loud. She was sure it had to be Lenny! That familiar laugh, the way Spirit brought them together, and the dark Spirit he carried with him.

CHAPTER THREE

Marie, Charleston

Marie sat on the veranda drinking a glass of wine. She thought this big old house was too quiet without her grandmother, Leona. Her presence was so big that it felt like three people were living there instead of two. Marie missed those two personalities, she smiled as she made that analogy.

"Hello, Marie, Are you decent?"

Marie heard someone yelling and glanced over the railing, "Dora, please come up."

Dora was one of her grandmother's oldest and dearest friends. When she appeared it was like a mini hurricane blew in, talk about overwhelming personalities. She made her way up the wrought iron stairs to the balcony. "My dear, I've come to kidnap you for dinner," Dora said excitedly.

"This isn't another setup, Dora? Is it? I remember that last dinner you talked me into," Marie asked.

"Nooo, my dear, this is purely a girl's night out. I was going to call Martha also. Are you game?"

Marie thought for a minute, "Okay, let's call Martha. I'm in," she said, finishing her glass of wine.

The women made plans to meet at Dora's favorite restaurant the Charleston Grill in an hour.

"Marie, have you heard from our dear Leona lately?" Dora asked.

"Not since she called to say she arrived safely. And that she made a new friend on the flight."

Marie went on to explain about Leona's new friend while she poured them both a glass of wine.

"New friend?" Dora asked with a smile.

Marie went on to explain about Leona's new friend, "It seems that Aunt Florence was quite taken with him, even though he was my age. She is such a flirt with all young men. Haven't you noticed that with Christian and Boyd?

"She is, but it's all in good fun. That woman sure knows how to have fun!" Dora said with admiration.

"Yes, but it can be very embarrassing, " Marie said; as she took the last sip of her wine and suggested they be on their way to the restaurant.

Martha was waiting for them when they arrived. The waitress led them to Dora's favorite table. It had the greatest vantage point for people watching, and Dora loved to keep up on local comings and goings.

"Marie, you're looking well. Dora, my dear, it's been too long," Martha said as she embraced them both.

"You're looking pretty spiffy with that new haircut, Aunt Martha," Marie said. The two discovered that they were related when a Spirit brought together Leona and Martha a few years back. It came to light that Leona's husband, Herbert, and Martha shared the same great-great-grandfather. So somewhere in that lineage Martha and Marie are distantly related.

"Yes, I love it!" Dora agreed.

"So, what's the occasion?" Martha asked, knowing Dora always had an ulterior motive.

"Well, we haven't been together, just the three of us in a while….." Dora tried to explain.

"Right, Dora, we know better! What's up?" Marie asked.

Dora went on to explain, "I already knew about Lenny," She gave Marie a sad look as if to say sorry I should have told you. Leona had called her and asked if they could do a bit of sleuthing with Martha's help at the courthouse. Dora took out a piece of paper from her purse, laid it on the table, and looked at them both. It was all the information Leona had gathered on Lenny. She looked at Marie and Martha.

"What do you say?" Dora asked anxiously.

"Why? What's so special about this guy?" Marie asked.

"Oh, I forgot to mention. Although Leona went to New Orleans with specific intentions of no Spirit encounters, Spirit had other plans," she laughed, "There's a message."

"What! Tell us," asked Martha excitedly.

"Leona heard, *'You are here to help him.'* She's not sure what that means but there's one other clue. His laugh, she said it's familiar," Dora said, shrugging her shoulders.

Marie and Martha looked over the piece of paper with all the information. It wasn't much to go on but they could start. It seemed Lenny Renard was about Marie's age so they could narrow that down. Plus he was in the Air Force, out of Barksdale.

"With him being from New Orleans it might limit my ability to find anything, but I'll try," Martha said.

"I have a friend who just finished their internship with me that's in the Air Force Reserves. I can ask him which direction to go in. But being military, that information might be hard to come by," Marie offered.

"The Renard family name is French. I have some friends that may be able to help also," Dora added.

They finished their lunch and made plans to meet the following week to compare notes.

CHAPTER FOUR

Grace, New Orleans

Flo and Leona found a seat at an outdoor table in the courtyard. The breeze was just enough to cut the humidity that was creeping in off the river. And the shade from the oaks helped block the afternoon sun.

Cafe Amelie had the best shrimp and grits as far as Flo was concerned. She recommended it to Leona as they both looked at the menus while waiting for Grace.

"Ladies, so good to see you," Grace said smiling, as she bent over to kiss Leona's cheek.

"My, you look wonderful! What keeps you looking so young?" Leona laughed.

"Actually, it's Mahalia's Place. I truly believe Granny watches over us," Grace said.

The ladies exchanged small talk and turned to the menus. Once again Flo encouraged the shrimp and grits. Grace leaned towards the gumbo. Leona immediately knew what she wanted, ahi tuna. The waitress brought water and a basket of bread and took their orders.

It had been a year and a half since Leona had been back to New Orleans. She missed the feeling of home, even though it wasn't her's in this lifetime. Grace being there reminded her of our different timelines and how eventually they do interconnect.

Grace caught them up on the expansion of her business. She had acquired five more properties and was in the process of refurbishing them. Although one had to be totally demolished, they tried to save it, and it broke her heart that she couldn't. Before she would allow the demolition to start, Grace tracked down the original owners before Katrina. They would give her the history of the house and hopefully their blessing. She would never level a home unless absolutely necessary. The ladies understood this as they all knew these homes were Spirits themselves. They all had stories to tell.

"As I refurbish or rebuild, I place a small plaque on each house with a number. This number links it to Mahalia's Place where I keep all the history of each individual house we have worked on."

"What a wonderful way of preserving the history of these neighborhoods!" Leona said.

"I actually had one family come back recently when they found out we were working on their old house. It was such a wonderful feeling seeing them reunited."

"I would love to see your work. Can we take a ride over sometime this week? That's if you have time?" Leona asked.

Grace laughed, "Of course, any time! I can always use a break. Flo knows where we are, just give me a call ahead of time and I'll give you the grand tour."

After their meal, the ladies decided to stroll over to Jackson Square. The streets weren't crowded yet and there were plenty of benches in the square. As they sat in the shade of an old magnolia, Grace reminded them of the afternoon she had heard her house's Spirit. Which led her to meet Leona and Maggie, who were visiting Flo.

Leona sighed as she sat down, "There's so much old history here. Every time I come I feel it, so sad."

"Those are the times that I wish we didn't have the sight. But we do, so we do the best we can to help," Flo said.

It was just at that moment that they heard him laugh! Leona spun around to look behind her. There stood Lenny, laughing at a young child who was doing cartwheels on the lawn. She looked over to Flo.

"That's Lenny, do you hear that laugh?" She got up and headed for him. Calling his name, he recognized her and met her halfway.

"Leona, hi! Wow, how are you?" he said, kissing her cheek.

Leona introduced him to Grace as he hugged Flo, "How's my flirty friend, Miss Flo?"

"Oh, You bad boy," Flo said, winking.

They all sat together chatting, Lenny learned about Mahalia's Place from Grace and seemed very interested. He was a subcontractor with a construction company in Charleston. That's why he was flying back when he met Leona. His project had just finished up and he had been looking forward to some downtime. But the idea of revitalizing his hometown appealed to him.

"Grace, if you are ever in need of a construction engineer I'd love to help," Lenny said.

"Oh my, are you kidding? Really?" A stunned Grace said, almost afraid of the answer.

"Absolutely, I just need a few weeks off to recharge. But after that I'm all yours until the next contract comes through," he said.

Grace and Lenny exchanged cell numbers and promised to stay in touch. Leona was sure this is what her message meant. She was sure of it. Her only question was why did that laugh sound so familiar?

CHAPTER FIVE

Marie, Charleston

It had been a week since Marie, Dora, and Martha went to lunch. They each had their assignment on finding out more about Lenny Renard for Leona. Marie had promised to contact a friend who was in the military to find out what she could. She was anxious to hear what the others had found out.

The ladies decided to meet at Cafe Framboise on Market Street for brunch instead of lunch. Martha arrived first and got a table. Dora's whirlwind arrival was followed closely by Marie. Each one wanted to speak first, and did until the waitress asked for their order.

"Oh my, we haven't even looked at the menu," Marie laughed.

After making their decisions they called the waitress back over, apologizing. They all decided to make it easy, Quiche Lorraine, which was the best there! Martha and Dora ordered coffee while Marie ordered orange juice.

"I've had too much coffee this morning, one more cup and I'll float away," she laughed, "so who goes first?"

"Since you asked, why don't you," Dora said.

Marie was more than happy to tell them what she found out. There was indeed an Air Force base in Barksdale,

Louisiana. And B52s did fly out of there. Chances are that Lenny worked there at one time or another. Her friend had found Leonard Renard who was stationed there about five years ago. He was married and discharged under hardship; that record was sealed.

"Leona said that Lenny had no wife or girlfriend, maybe there's more than one. Or he could have been stationed at another base," Marie offered, looking at the other women.

"Well, I found a Renard family right here in Charleston!" Martha blurted out.

"Did they have a son Leonard?" Dora asked.

"No, just two girls, Abigail and Cecilia," she said sadly.

Dora was surprisingly quiet, she was lost in her thoughts.

"Dora, can you add anything?" Martha asked.

She knew what she wanted to say but was afraid of getting everyone's hopes up. She had indeed found the same family Martha had. They had moved out of Charleston about twenty-five years ago and there was a scandal.

"I think I know who Lenny's mother might be….."

Before she could continue Marie said, "What tell us!"

Dora told them the story of Cecilia Renard, "Cecilia was just sixteen when she got pregnant. She refused to name the father, swearing she didn't know. It happened at a party and unfortunately, she was drunk. The family picked up and moved to…..."

"New Orleans!!!" Marie and Martha yelled out in unison.

"Yes, I think they had family there. It devastated the family, I thought she put the baby up for adoption, but I guess not."

"Leona will be surprised by the amount of information we found. Who's going to tell her?" asked Martha.

"Dora, she confided in you. You get to tell her," Marie said.

CHAPTER SIX

Cecilia, New Orleans

Leona had been in New Orleans for two weeks now and wasn't a bit homesick. She was thoroughly enjoying her time with her sister. They had managed to run into Lenny another time at Cafe du Monde. It seemed that everyone who lived in the Quarter headed to the cafe every morning. Some days during the tourist season the lines were out the doors. Flo knew the best times to go, early, which led to morning walks along the river. They would walk down to the Aquarium after beignets at least three times a week.

"What do you think of Dora's discovery back in Charleston?" Flo asked.

"I'm hoping that Lenny doesn't think we are stalking him. I don't want him to know we are investigating him, it's kind of creepy. But I know there's more to him than just helping Grace," Leona said looking concerned.

"We both know there is a sad Spirit around him, I feel that it's one he can't let go of. He's keeping it here," said Flo.

As the two women walked, they discussed how they could find out more information in New Orleans about Lenny's family history. Flo suggested that Grace might be a help. With her connections at the courthouse, they could dig deeper. Leona agreed and planned on calling Grace later that day.

As they rounded the corner to the condo Leona's cell phone rang.

"Leona, it's Marie, I've got news," she said excitedly.

"All right, hang on, let me put you on speaker. Flo's right here. Okay, go."

Marie told them about Martha's friend from the census board. It turned out he was a professional genealogist! He plugged in Cecilia's name and her family tree came up. They did indeed move to New Orleans; some of the family still lived there. But the exciting part was that Leonard Renard was attached to Cecilia. She was his mother, and she was alive!

"Marie, that's unbelievable. Tell Martha she did great work!"

"I'll email you the family tree so you guys can take it from there. I just hope this guy is open to your Spirit," Marie said.

"Me, too, sweetheart. Me, too. Talk to you soon," said Leona.

As the ladies entered Flo's condo they found Geraldine sitting at the kitchen table. The table was set for four.

Looking at Geraldine, Flo said, "What's going on daughter? We weren't expecting you, let alone someone else."

"Sorry, Mom, but a friend of mine wanted to meet you and Aunt Leona. It seems that you all have a mutual friend," Geraldine said mysteriously.

There was a knock at the door as if right on cue. Leona looked at Flo and shrugged her shoulders as if to say, what the heck, bring it on. Geraldine opened the door and a stunning woman stood in the doorway. The rose-colored dress fit like a glove, and matching shoes and clutch purse completed her outfit. The double strand of pearls around her neck said she was from money as did her demeanor. She kissed Geraldine on both cheeks and turned toward the ladies.

"Leona, Florence, so nice to finally meet you. I've been waiting a long time. My name is Cecilia Fiord, formally Renard," she said as if she had known them for years.

The ladies stood there dumbfounded for a minute before recovering their whits.

"Oh my? How?" Flo said.

Geraldine directed them all into the kitchen where they sat. Leona remembered seeing the bottle of Four Roses bourbon on the table previously. Now she understood why. If this was Spirit, she knew they were in for a wild ride.

Cecilia took a deep breath and looked at Geraldine, who nodded and she began. "First, let me apologize for coming unannounced but Spirit assured me it was the right time," she paused.

Leona and Flo looked at each other, not believing what they were hearing.

"I am Leonard's mother, you probably know that by now. My son has lived in a dark place for the past two years. Geraldine tells me you both are sensitive to Spirit. When Leonard told me of two crazy old ladies he met at the airport I knew they finally sent you!"

"Old!!" Flo said, "Wait till I see him, I'll give him old!"

"He did say you flirted with him shamelessly," Cecilia laughed.

"Cecilia, who finally sent us? And why have you been waiting?" Leona asked.

"Geraldine, can I have two fingers please," Cecilia said, pointing to the bourbon? "I have been visited by Spirit since I was a teenager. Sometimes I listened, most times it scared me. But at all times she was right. I had Leonard out of wedlock but that's another story. Right now I need your help with him. Geraldine tells me that you felt the female Spirit around him," she paused as they both nodded, afraid to break the spell.

"Leonard was married five years ago while he was in the Air Force. His wife, Jade, was the love of his life. They were so happy. He was overseas when it happened, a car accident. She was killed and he has never gotten over it. I fear that he won't let her move on. I have tried my best to help him but he just keeps running from one city to the next on jobs. Six months ago Spirit told me help was coming. I assume that is you," she said looking at Flo and Leona.

"I feel the darkness around him, you're right. I think he's holding her here. How can we help?"Leona asked.

"Hasn't Spirit told you?" Cecilia responded.

"No, not yet. Maybe she was waiting for us to meet," Leona giggled.

CHAPTER SEVEN

Marie, Charleston

It was early Saturday morning before the sun came up. A noise woke her. Being alone in this big old house gave her the willies. She listened again for any movement. Thinking the noise must have been outside. Marie decided to get up even though it was only 5:30. Throwing on her robe and slippers she headed down to the kitchen for coffee. The sound of creaking stairs gave her a sense of comfort, of home. After making herself a cup of coffee she decided to watch the sunrise from the veranda. Marie sat on the wrought iron chair and placed the cup on the table when she heard it again.

It was a muffled noise like someone was talking in a low voice. She stood up and looked down into the courtyard. Once Spirit had her attention she heard, ***"He needs you, go."*** Of course, Spirit would make sure she had her attention, Marie laughed. Go? Where, she wondered, who needed me? She knew that Spirit would open the doors that needed to be opened. Marie drank her coffee and prepared herself for a day at work. Wondering all the while when her next hint would come.

Marie had been blessed by the Goddesses with her job. After graduating last year, a local architectural company sought her out after she had won a design award. She landed a job without even looking for one! And the best part was, it was within walking distance from home. Her day usually started with a meeting. Proposals and projects were presented. The staff would report where they stood on their jobs. But this morning turned out just a bit different.

Sarah, her boss had texted her, 'I need to see you.'

Marie wondered, did I screw something up, as she walked down the hall to Sarah's office?

"Marie, please sit. I have a favor to ask you," Sarah said. As Marie sat down in front of her desk, she continued, "I realize that you've only been with us a little over a year but I have full confidence that you are up to this task. We have a proposal from a company just outside New Orleans. I need eyes on the site before I agree to the project. I know you have family there and thought, if you would agree, I'd give you a few weeks to visit with them after checking out the project."

"Oh my, yes! That sounds wonderful. But, Sarah, I've never done this before," Marie questioned.

"There's always a first time for everything. This would be a big boost to your career and I'm confident you can do it. Remember, you have all the resources you need at your fingertips."

"When would you need me to go?" Marie asked.

"I'd like to take a couple of days to prepare you, how about two days from today? There's one more thing, the project manager from New Orleans is here. He'd like to go over things before you go to the actual site. I thought that would be a good idea. He leaves the day after tomorrow so I'd like for you to free up your afternoon."

"Great, I'll call my great aunt. I can stay with her while I'm there. That will save the company money on hotels," Marie said smiling.

"I'll have my secretary make your flight arrangements and a rental car, you'll need that," Sarah said, shaking Marie's hand.

"Thank you, Sarah, for this opportunity."

Marie knew it was Spirit, who else could have coordinated this scenario so well? She would go, and she already guessed it was Lenny who needed her. There was no other 'He' in her life.

Stopping by the breakroom on her way to her office she grabbed a cup of coffee. As she was pouring the coffee she heard Spirit again, ***"He needs you, go."***

Not realizing, she responded out loud, "Geez, I can only go so fast. I'll get there."

"I'm sorry, I didn't mean to pressure you. I can wait," a co-worker said.

Turning, she saw a handsome man with dark hair and a beard. Just for a second, she thought she recognized him.

"No, no, it's not you. I'm so sorry. I was talking to myself. Totally unrelated to coffee," she said apologetically, laughing nervously, "You must think I'm crazy."

"Actually, no. I understand, stress and all. By the way, I'm Randy," he said.

"Hi, I'm Marie. Are you new here?" she asked, realizing she hadn't seen him before.

"Yes and no. Sounds convoluted," he laughed, "I just recently flew in from New Orleans. I'm meeting with a project assistant this afternoon on a new proposal."

Marie just stared at him, she couldn't remember Spirit ever pushing so hard. She debated whether to tell him or not that she was his project assistant. I need time to absorb this. She quickly made an excuse for being late for a meeting. And left him standing there looking confused. Marie had one thing on her mind, she had to talk to her grandmother, Leona.

As she closed the door to her office and headed to her desk, the phone rang. After staring at it for a few seconds, afraid to answer, thinking it could be Leona, she answered.

"Hello," she said in a whisper.

"Marie, why are you whispering? Did I catch you at a bad time?" Maggie asked.

"Oh, Maggie. Thank goodness it's you," Marie said, breathing easier. She explained why she was whispering and about her message from Spirit. Maggie called to see if she could join her and Christian for dinner that night.

"I know you're not cooking with Aunt Leona away. Come eat with us tonight. I invited Martha, too. She's bringing her Carolina Sweet Wine," Maggie said, trying to entice her.

"That sounds great, yes. What time?"

"How about seven, that gives everyone time to get home from work," Maggie replied.

With plans made for later on, Marie relaxed. Things were happening faster than she was used to. Talking to Leona would help, she thought as she punched in the numbers on her cell phone.

As it turned out Leona was just finishing up her breakfast beignet and coffee at Cafe du Monde when the phone rang. Flo had woken up with a headache so Leona decided to take her coffee and walk alone. Marie filled her in on Spirit's activities and demands. In turn, Leona told her about meeting Cecilia and her concerns for Lenny.

"Gran, do you think it's Lenny that Spirit wants me to help?"

"It sure seems that way. Tell me about this Randy person, is he cute?" Leona asked.

"He's just a co-worker…..but there was a split-second moment that he looked familiar," Marie admitted.

Leona laughed, "Remember who's directing you, child."

The morning went by without further distractions. Marie checked her watch to make sure she was ready for her meeting with Sarah and Randy. She had just enough time to grab a salad for lunch.

The conference room was chilly when Marie sat down. I should have brought my sweater, she thought, folding her arms in front of her. Sarah and Randy came in a few minutes later laughing. It seemed that they already had a working relationship through their banter.

Seeing Marie sitting at the table, Randy's eyes opened wide. He whispered, "Why didn't you tell me this morning?"

Marie smiled sweetly and shrugged her shoulders.

As Sarah opened her notebook, Randy stood and took off his jacket. Walking over to Marie, he said, "You are making me cold just watching you, please take my jacket."

"No, I mean thank you. I'll just go get my sweater, thank you…." she stammered backing out the door.

Oh, my Goddess, I just made a fool of myself, she thought. Quickly grabbing her sweater she hurried back to the conference room. Randy was standing over blueprints pointing to an area he looked concerned about. Sarah was nodding agreement as she signaled Marie to join them.

"Randy's company has come up with a beautiful complex for our client's project, but we have a slight problem," Sarah said.

"I'm sure we can rectify it, our engineers are working on it as we speak," Randy replied.

Sarah filled Marie in on the pertinent information she would need to evaluate the situation once she was on site. They discussed the plans for the next two hours, Sarah's expectations, and Randy's solutions. Marie felt like a volleyball, going from one side to another.

Sarah's secretary knocked on the door, "Sorry to interrupt. I can't get a flight out until after the weekend for Marie. Which day do you prefer?" She said looking at Marie.

Before she could answer Randy interrupted, "Please, join me. I have the company jet at my disposal. I'll be going back the day after tomorrow if that's okay with you."

Marie looked at Sarah who nodded, "If it's okay with you Marie, that will be fine. Thank you, Randy."

"Fine, that's fine," Marie managed to get out. Before she knew what she was saying she asked, "Since you're being so nice can I interest you in dinner tonight? My friends are having a small dinner party."

"That would be great, I was just going to grab something at the hotel," he said.

Sarah wrapped up the meeting. She told Marie they would meet in the morning to firm up all the details. Smiling at Randy, she winked at Marie and left the conference room.

"If you give me the address I can meet you there. I have another meeting at three. What time is this shindig?" asked Randy.

Marie gave him the time and address, then headed back to her office. What have I done? Am I crazy? she thought.

CHAPTER EIGHT

Lenny, New Orleans

Lenny sat on the second floor of The Lighthouse Bar and Grill gazing out the window. He remembered the first time he met her, it was here. Jade had been visiting with her family. The bar was in an RV park located on the canal that connects Lake Pontchartrain to the Mississippi River. He had been doing some construction work on new bulkheads along the canal. His crew suggested stopping in at the bar for a drink after work. She was sitting with her family at a table when he saw her. Their eyes locked for a split second before she looked away. It will be two years next week, he thought. It still seems like yesterday when I met you.

His thoughts went back to that day...... The clouds rolled in and the skies opened up while he was having a drink. He noticed the family had finished their dinner and were headed downstairs. Knowing how hard it was raining he decided to follow them. Maybe they would walk around the gift shop awhile. The rain was torrential, no one ventured out. He walked around until he spotted her again. She was looking at postcards.

"Excuse me, could I recommend one?" Lenny asked.

She looked up, directly into his eyes. She took his breath away. "Yes, please."

Stumbling over his words he finally said, "This one, it's my favorite." Handing her a beautiful picture of St Louis Cathedral at sunset in Jackson Square.

"You're right, it's beautiful. My students will love it," she said smiling.

"Students? Are you a teacher, my goodness you look young enough to be in high school?"

As the rain continued, Lenny and Jade got to know each other. Finding a bench on the porch they listened to the rain as they talked. She was visiting with her mom and dad in their RV. They were retired. It was spring break from the school she worked at. And her parents asked her to join them for a few days. They all lived in Tampa, Florida, and hadn't visited New Orleans before.

He explained how he was in the Air Force, crew chief on a B52. But his love was construction, he was taking classes for his engineering degree. His crew visited MacDill Air Base, which was in Tampa, occasionally when assisting in exercises in refueling the KC135. New Orleans was his home, he was here on leave helping a buddy build bulkheads. He only had a few more days then back to Barksdale, which was about three hundred miles north.

As the rain slowed, Jade's father let her know he was headed back to the RV with her mother. After introducing Lenny to her parents, Jade asked Lenny if he had time for a drink. They spent the next three hours talking. It was like nothing Lenny had ever experienced. He didn't want it to end. They made plans for dinner the following night. It was then that they both realized they wanted a relationship.

Lenny went back to Barksdale and Jade went back to Tampa. They spoke as often as they could, sometimes for hours in the evenings. Jade took long weekends with her parents' RV and drove to Barksdale. Lenny volunteered for overnight trips to MacDill just to see her.

It only took six months before he proposed and another three months before they were married. Jade moved to Barksdale and got a job at the daycare center on base. They thought it would be very convenient for when they had children. Jade talked of having two or three children. She had been an only child and felt she missed out on having a sibling. Lenny agreed, as he also was an only child. He knew the loneliness when there was no one to play with. His mother used to tell him he was lucky, he got all the attention.

After they were married a year Lenny and Jade decided to start a family. They talked of names and colors for the nursery over dinners, on drives, and pretty much all the time. After six months went by and Jade wasn't pregnant she visited the doctor. They ran tests and determined that both were able to conceive. But she did have scarring from endometriosis which would make it harder than normal. After the shock wore off, Lenny used to tease her that practice makes perfect, and their child would be perfect.

Their life together was perfect in Lenny's eyes, he loved her more each day. His missions took him overseas for short periods. During those times Jade would visit her parents in Tampa. It was in September, he was away. A hurricane warning went up for the west coast of Florida. Jade went to her parent's home to help them prepare for the storm. She left later than usual, it was dark by the time she got to Tampa. The outer bands of the storm were pelting her car. Headlights were coming at her, her car swerved, hit another car, and rolled.

Lenny spent the next year in mental isolation. He went on with life from the outside but refused help or condolences from anyone. He cut himself off from friends and refused to see his mother. Jade's parents reached out to him numerous times; he refused to see them. He spent his time off sitting in the nursery she had decorated. He drank more than he should have and knew it.

After six months his base commander recommended a hardship discharge. He didn't fight it. There was nothing to fight for. Jade's life insurance money left him very well off, he didn't need to find a job. He did, however, have to move out of his base housing. There would be no children with Jade, leaving that nursery was the first step to separation. He moved back to New Orleans and rented an apartment on Jackson Square where he could see the cathedral. Once he was back he threw himself into finding long-distance construction jobs.

It was after the first anniversary of her death that he heard her say, ***"Live my love, let me go."*** He was folding his laundry and turned around expecting to see her. When he didn't he questioned his sanity. Was it just wishful thinking? He remembered his mother telling him about Spirit and how when we need things the most, Spirit helps us find our way. He knew where he had to go.

"Mama, I need you," Lenny said, as she opened her front door.

He poured his heart out for hours. Cecilia listened, hugged, and wiped his tears. She made him his favorite catfish dinner and they shared a bit of bourbon. He fell asleep exhausted on her couch. She kissed his cheek, covered him with a blanket, and thanked the Goddesses that brought him back to her.

CHAPTER NINE

Randy

Randy was a bit of a snob, having grown up privileged. His family home sat on the Thames River in Connecticut, with views you could see in famous magazines. His mother wasn't the typical socialite; her time was spent doing charity work. She never fit in with the club wives, her friends were more common people. She often told Randy that his true friends would find him.

Randy excelled in high school which led to a degree from Yale. His father's firm hired him after graduating. Randy's job was troubleshooting projects, he seemed to have the ability to see problems before they occurred. Which led him to Charleston.

He was a little nervous about dinner tonight, was this a date? I hope not, he thought. That would make working together messy and he hated drama. He rang the bell just as Marie walked up beside him.

"Fancy meeting you here," she laughed.

"I guess I'm at the right place," he answered as the door opened.

"Come in, please. Marie, good to see you. Who have we here," Maggie said as she kissed Marie's cheek.

"I'm Randy, I hope it's alright, Marie invited me," he said holding his hand out. He had never seen such jet-black hair. Realizing he was staring, he looked away.

"Of course, I'm Maggie." Sensing him starring, she said, "Come meet the others."

Marie made the introductions, first Martha, then Christian. Randy had never seen such an eclectic group of people. Each person had their own ethnicity, strange. His friends all consisted of what people called wasps, White Anglo-Saxton Protestants.

As Maggie poured cocktails she felt Randy's discomfort. "Randy, where do you hail from?"

"Connecticut, I grew up there," he stammered, not understanding why he was so uncomfortable. They seemed like nice people, why was he feeling like this? "My father is from Texas, he moved to Connecticut to marry my mother."

"How romantic," Martha gushed.

"That's true love," Christian said, looking at his wife.

"How do you like Charleston?" Martha asked.

"I really haven't seen anything except Marie's office. My jet flew in this morning," They all looked at him strangely, "Not mine, the company jet," he stammered.

Dinner was a bit strained, to say the least. Maggie was hoping a few cocktails would relax him, but it didn't work until Martha started telling her story.

"Randy, did you know Maggie is my great-great grandniece?" she said laughing.

"What?" he said, looking from Martha to Maggie.

"My kin were slaves. My great-great-grandfather and Herbert, Leona's husband's great-great-grandfather are the same. It appeared he had a liking for many women. After the Civil War, our grandfathers worked together and built a successful company. But then things changed and my father had to go away. As it turned out he left me very wealthy, thanks to Leona and Maggie unearthing these family secrets. Now we are family, no matter what color our skin," Martha said smiling.

"Wait, how about me? My daddy was Leona's son. I'm her granddaughter. My momma was a slave descendant, from the Gullah community. That's why I'm light brown," Marie said, giggling.

Now everyone was laughing and talking, "Maggie, tell him," Christian said.

She looked at Randy who nodded with enthusiasm. "I'm from New Orleans, my momma and grand-mere are French creole Goddesses," she laughed, "My jet black hair comes from my divine feminine line."

Randy was awestruck…..he had never met so many different people. And so proud of their families. It made him sad that he never experienced this kind of love.

"Christian, what's your story?" Randy asked inquisitively.

"Which lifetime?" he replied as the room broke into cheers, "Sorry, Randy, that's a whole different story."

The evening continued with questions and answers. He wanted to meet this woman Leona, she seemed to be at the heart of each story. By the end of the evening, Randy didn't want to leave, he felt at home…which was very unusual for him.

CHAPTER TEN

Marie

The sun peeked through the curtains just enough to wake her before the alarm. Marie rolled over, hit the off button, and sat on the side of the bed. She watched the dust particles dance in the beam of sunlight for a moment. Oh my goodness, I'm going to New Orleans tomorrow! Realizing that she hadn't packed a thing she decided to venture into the attic for a suitcase. Sliding her feet into slippers she headed to the hallway.

Marie pulled the staircase down from the ceiling. She hated going up in that attic, especially alone. But, the suitcases weren't coming down on their own. Grabbing the rails she ventured up, switching on the light she sat on the edge. As she looked around she noticed a small square case, it appeared to be very old. Thinking it would be great for her makeup she grabbed that and another larger suitcase. Slowly sliding them down the stairs in front of her. As she neared the bottom she let them drop. The small case opened up and pictures and letters flew everywhere.

Marie quickly closed up the staircase to the ceiling and collected the pictures. Stuffing them back into the case she grabbed the larger one and headed to her bedroom. Sitting down on the bed Marie opened the small case. There were pictures and a letter, and the woman looked familiar. She looked over each picture, realizing they were of her mother, Fatu. Then she found one with the two of them, her mother and father. They were so young, and so opposite, him with his skin so white and hers so dark. You could see even then how much he loved her. Why were these in the attic? Why hadn't Nana given them to her? Or her father when she finally did meet him.

As she sat deep in thought, a single tear rolled down her cheek for the people she never really knew. The cell phone alarm startled her, it was her 'fifteen-minute till I have to leave for work reminder. Stuffing the pictures and letter back into the case she raced to the shower.

The day continued to be a whirlwind, meetings with Sarah, agenda rescheduling of her projects here in Charleston, and making arrangements for closing up the house. Marie knew she could count on Dora for that job. There wasn't much to do except take in the mail and water the plants, thankfully there were no pets to look after.

Sarah's secretary appeared at her office door, "Marie, I have your itinerary," she said handing the paper to her. "Mr. Winslow's jet leaves at nine tomorrow morning. I have a car picking you up at eight-fifteen from your home. The rental car company has a kiosk at the airport with transportation to their office. Now about your return flight, you'll have to call me when you know you're coming home. Sarah told me it would be a few weeks, I'll make all your arrangements then," she said smiling.

"Thank you so much, this is great. You've thought of everything," Marie replied.

Marie took the next half hour talking to Leona, "Nana, I hope it's not an imposition having me come. Are you sure Auntie Flo has room?"

"Oh child, you know Flo. The more the merrier!" Leona replied.

"I'm looking forward to seeing Geraldine, too, it's been a while. You know I'll be busy the first couple of days with my project so don't plan anything big."

"No, dear. Just a small gathering of my closest hundred friends," Leona said laughing.

"Nana, I've missed your laughter. I'll see you soon. Love you,"

Marie stopped at the deli on her way home and picked up a sub sandwich. Once again the big house felt so empty as she came in the back door. Setting her purse down she unwrapped the sub and took a beer out of the refrigerator. Standing there at the counter, eating the sandwich, she thought, I can't wait for some home-cooked jambalaya and a muffuletta!

Since she didn't know how long this trip was going to be, Marie packed casual and dress clothes. Her mind was on a million other things as she stuffed everything into the large suitcase. Good thing I found that makeup case, she thought as she piled her toiletries on top of the forgotten pictures. Going over the list in her mind, she felt confident she had packed everything she needed. Grabbing a suitcase in each hand she took them downstairs. And sat them near the front door, ready for the morning.

CHAPTER ELEVEN

Leona, New Orleans

Leona was so excited, Marie was coming. She missed her granddaughter. Although they lived together now, it was only a few short years ago that they were made aware of each other's existence. Ronald, Leona's son, had a daughter. He didn't know about her until she appeared in his office one day. Since then Leona and Marie have been trying to make up for the lost time.

Up till now, Marie was the only one who knew the secret Leona had been hiding, it was time she told Flo. Maybe today's the day, Leona thought, I'll tell her on our walk.

"Flo…you ready?" Leona yelled to her sister.

"I'm coming, it takes time to make this old lady presentable," Flo yelled back from the bathroom.

"It's only a walk for heaven's sake. You're going to be all sweaty shortly anyway, shake a leg."

Flo came out of the bathroom decked out in bright green yoga pants and a tee-shirt that was tie-dyed from the seventies. A matching bright green bandana was wrapped around her head.

Leona took one look at her and burst out laughing, "Oh my Goddess! Where did you get that outfit? I think the seventies are calling and they want it back!"

"I love it! I knew this would come back into style. I have another outfit in orange if you want to match me," she giggled.

"In what world, sister? Well, at least I won't lose you in a crowd!" Leona said, laughing even harder.

Their morning walk ended up being one for the books. Several young girls stopped them along the way. They loved Flo's outfit and wanted to know where she bought it. Which made Flo feel justified in her decision to wear it. More mature walkers just smiled and giggled as they pointed to her behind her back. Leona made her promise never to wear that outfit again.

"There are my girls," Lenny said, catching up to them as they walked past the aquarium. "Flo, I spotted you way back by the riverboat. I was jogging along and saw these bright green legs. I thought to myself, that could only be one person," he said trying to catch his breath.

"Are you sure it was the green legs and not two crazy old ladies!" Flo said trying to sound intimidating.

"Oh my, I see you met my mother. That was said with much respect. You guys are the best!" Lenny said trying to butter up Flo.

"Lenny, don't listen to that old bat, she knows exactly what you meant," Leona said laughing.

"Come give me a hug. Yes, we met your mother. Such a sweet woman. All is forgiven," Flo said, smiling.

The three strolled along the riverfront. Leona asked Lenny if he was going to be in town the next few days. "My granddaughter, Marie, is coming into town on business. I was wondering if you could join us for dinner one night. I would love to invite your mother also."

"Do you really want us to intrude on a family dinner?"

"Lenny, we consider our friends as family…you know crazy old ladies and all," Flo giggled.

"Then, I would be honored," he said bowing mockingly, "I've got to run now ladies, literally, finish up my jog," he said as he hugged them both.

A few thunder clouds rolled in and Flo suggested they turn back. She knew it was coming, not just the rain. But another kind of storm, one more personal. They got back to the condo just as the skies opened up. Drying themselves off, Leona put the kettle on for tea. She busied herself with setting out the cups and a few leftover muffins.

"So, how long are you going to drag this out, sister?" Flo said.

Leona looked at her and laughed, "I should have known I couldn't keep this from you."

The sisters sat down to tea. The news wasn't good. Flo knew Leona was hiding health issues but wasn't sure what it was. The diagnosis was terminal. Leona got the news six months ago. The doctors said the treatment would slow the progression but not cure it. Dr. Reynolds encouraged her to start treatment immediately. For Leona there was no question, after careful consideration, she opted for no treatment.

She explained her decision to Flo, "The treatment will make me sicker than I already am. Right now I am doing okay, I have my off days. But what days I have left I want to enjoy, not be centered around doctors and treatments."

"Oh, sister. I support your decision one hundred percent. We both know that when it's our time to join Source and the

Divine Feminine we will be welcomed home by Spirit. We will meet again dear one, in another lifetime, just as before," Flo said with tears in her eyes.

"Yes, that is why I wanted to be with you now. I need your help telling the others. I fear Dora will take this rather hard. Our beliefs are the same, but when the heart plays into them, it's harder to accept. She was the one who helped me through Ronald's death when I got lost. Our daughters and granddaughters have grown stronger in our beliefs, they will help you." Leona said, squeezing Flos' hand as they both cried.

CHAPTER TWELVE

Randy

Randy gazed out the window of the jet. The flight had been smooth. His conversation with Marie was pleasant. She now busied herself with project business. He was lost in his thoughts about the evening he met her family. He was drawn to them, this Yankee who looked down on southerners suddenly felt more at home with them than with his own country club set. His parents would understand, after all, they weren't from that community originally. Maybe he'd give his father a call later. He had never bothered to ask his father about growing up in Texas. He realized then, that he didn't even know where his mother was from either. Suddenly it was important to him to know his roots.

"Randy….excuse me, Randy," Marie said, tapping his arm.

"Sorry, did you ask me something?"

"Yes, I didn't mean to interrupt your train of thought. Just wondering how close we were to landing?" asked Marie.

"Not long now, I can ask the pilot,"

"No, it's alright, just wondering," she said, sounding nervous.

Sensing her uneasiness, he attempted to calm her nerves. He spoke of the project site and their schedules for visiting it. As he went on describing their various lists of discrepancies, he didn't notice she was lost in her thoughts.

Marie knew he was talking because his hands were so animated. She didn't hear a word, what she heard was Spirit. She knew Nana was telling Auntie Flo of her diagnosis at this very moment. She felt the pain and hurt in their hearts.

It was then that Randy noticed a single tear roll down Marie's cheek. "Marie, please, don't be scared. I know this is a big project. It'll be okay," he said with such compassion that Marie burst into tears. He reached over and hugged her, "I'm sorry, I didn't mean to upset you. What can I do?" he said as he handed her his handkerchief.

She turned to face him and smiled, "It's not what you think, I'm sorry."

They looked into each other's eyes for a split second before Randy pulled away. He felt a jolt, a feeling like he'd looked into those eyes before.

Marie felt the same thing, she looked away. The feeling was so intense. She waited for some kind of message from Spirit, but nothing came.

Thankfully the pilot announced they would be landing in ten minutes. Randy and Marie busied themselves with preparing to land. As the jet landed Marie saw the staircase being readied for their arrival. The jet stopped and the steward opened the door, a blast of hot humid air faced them as they walked down the stairs. A limousine awaited with cooler air. Marie had decided on picking up her rental car later that day. All she wanted right now was to hug her Nana.

"Would you like to have lunch before I drop you off to get your car?" Randy asked.

"If you don't mind, I'd like to go straight to my aunt's condo."

"Sure, no problem. Just give the driver the address," he said as he lowered the glass separating them from the driver. Which she did. "Marie, I'm sorry I upset you," Randy said.

"No, it wasn't you. It's my Nana. She's ill," she stopped as if she'd said too much.

"Leona? Oh no….I feel like I know her already. Just listening to your stories the other night."

"I just need to be with her today. She was breaking the news to my Auntie Flo, I felt it on the flight. Their hearts were breaking ...." Suddenly knowing she was making no sense she stopped talking.

Randy looked at her questionably but said nothing. He accepted what she had to say, but was not sure that he understood what it meant.

The limo dropped Marie off at Flos's condo and Randy headed to his hotel. Unpacking his suitcase he thought back to her eyes. Why had they seemed so familiar? Pouring himself a drink he sat at the table and looked out the window. The Mississippi River shimmered just ever so slightly, he thought for a moment that he saw tiny fairies dancing on the water. He blinked twice, looked at his glass of bourbon, and thought, no more booze for me. He checked his watch and decided to call his mother.

"Hello, Winslow residence," Sue answered.

"Hello Sue, it's Randy. Is my mother home?"

"Mr. Randy, good to hear from you, your mother will be very happy to hear from you. Hold on."

"Son, is that you?"

"Yes mother, how are you?" he asked, feeling awkward.

"Talk to me boy! What's going on?"

Randy told her everything, Marie, her family, and finally her eyes. Then he asked her about his roots. Where did she come from? Did he have any family elsewhere? So many questions.

They spoke for an hour. She told him of her family from Texas. They had been sharecroppers for generations. She understood things that others didn't. Her Granny was a healer and taught her when she was a child. She found it ironic that she had to move to Connecticut to meet her beloved who was from just down the road apiece.

"Son, follow those fairies," his mother whispered.

"What? How?" Randy asked, confused.

"Just live son, just live. Momma loves you bunches. Come see me soon. I have to run," she blew kisses into the phone and hung up.

CHAPTER THIRTEEN

Marie

Marie ran up the stairs dragging her suitcase. Before she could knock, the door opened.

"Auntie Flo," Marie said, hugging her, "So good to see you, how's Nana?"

"She's sleeping right now, her news tuckered her out."

"I felt it! I knew she was telling you. How are you handling it?" Marie asked.

"If I didn't believe we'd meet again it would be a lot harder. I know Source will find a way for us to meet again, another lifetime. Of course, it's still hard to say goodbye in this lifetime," Flo said, trying to smile.

"Auntie Flo, there is so much I still have to learn. Will you and Nana teach me?"

"Absolutely, Geraldine will be happy to help also. She loves teaching our beliefs, especially the phases of Grandmother Moon, the Goddess Luna."

Marie was struck by how 'out there' Auntie Flo was being. For the past few years, much of these beliefs weren't said out loud. They were eluded to now and again but never really talked about. Maybe because Nana's time was short, they needed to pass on the teaching.

Flo had set out lunch for them both while they let Leona sleep. They spoke of new family and friends. Flo sensed Marie had more questions about relationships but didn't ask. That would be her sister's pleasure. Geraldine would be coming by after her shift at the gift shop; she also sensed the bad news.

After lunch, Marie helped Flo smudge the room from negative energy. Flo lit the bundle of sage and gently blew out the flame. As the smoke rose from the bundle, she repeated her mantra in each corner of the room, "Holy herbs cleanse this space, bring us wisdom, clarity, and healing. Blessed be."

"Marie, I see you made it," Leona said, surprising them both.

"Nana!" Marie ran to Leona's outstretched arms.

"It's alright child, you're here now. We can do this," Leona said, stepping back, and looking at Marie.

"Yes ma'am, we can!" Marie said, wiping the tears away with the back of her hand.

"Come sit, we will all talk. I see the smudging has begun."

The three of them sat holding hands and sniffing back their tears.

Geraldine arrived shortly before four o'clock carrying a bag that smelled so good it made Leona's stomach rumble.

"I didn't think y'all would be up to cooking, so I picked up muffulettas. I assume there's beer in the frig," Geraldine smiled.

"Auntie Gerry! I'm so glad to see you," Marie said as she hugged her.

Geraldine held Marie's shoulders gently away from her and said, "Marie, you get prettier every time I see you. Let me look at you."

Marie spun around like a child would, showing off a new dress. "I'm so glad Spirit brought me here. Once my input on the project is done my boss gave me a few weeks off."

Geraldine looked at Flo and Leona, "I do believe Spirit has made all the arrangements. But first, we eat!"

The ladies indulged in Leona's favorite sandwich in N'awlins, the muffuletta. Geraldine had it stuffed with extra olive salad just the way Leona liked them. A few beers later the ladies were relaxed enough that the bad news of the day was forgotten, for a while anyway. They chatted about Marie's project and career, and the extended family back in Charleston.

The morning sun awakened her only minutes before Marie's cell phone alarm buzzed, for a minute she thought she was back home. Then realizing where she was, her stomach got butterflies. This is a big day for me, she thought. I have to make decisions I've never made before, please Goddess give me clarity she thought as she put a quartz crystal into her pocket. Knowing they would be going to the job site she dressed in jeans and sneakers, no heels today. She combed her hair into a ponytail, applied some makeup, and headed for the kitchen.

"Good morning, coffee?" Flo asked.

"Yes, please. I'm so nervous."

"Marie, you'll be fine. Your boss wouldn't have sent you if she didn't think you could do the job," Flo said, handing her a cup of steaming coffee.

Taking a sip, Marie smiled, "Chicory?"

"Of course, is there any other way?" Flo laughed.

Marie suddenly realized that she hadn't picked up her rental car! "Auntie Flo, how am I going to get to the job site? I'm to meet Randy there in thirty minutes?"

Flo gulped down her coffee, "I'm ready when you are!"

"Thank you, I guess things got away from me last night," Marie said, frowning.

"No time for regrets. This is a big day, let's go 'wow' your boss!!"

CHAPTER FOURTEEN

Randy

The morning was beautiful with hints of humidity in the air. A slight breeze rolled in off the river as a barge floated by being pushed by a tugboat. Randy walked to the project job site awaiting Marie. He was drawn to her but didn't need the drama of a long-distance romance. Plus it wasn't a good thing to mix business and pleasure. He would keep his distance today, all business.

Flo stopped the car at the curb, "Dang, that's one handsome man!"

"That's Randy. He's working on the project with me," Marie said shyly.

Flo raised one cyebrow, smiled, and said, "Enjoy your day."

"Thanks, I'll see you tonight," Marie said, closing the car door behind her.

Randy spotted her walking through the grass. Lord, she was beautiful! She looked like a teenager in jeans and a ponytail, how was he ever going to get through this day?

"Good morning," she yelled while waving at him.

"Hey, morning. I see you're dressed for work," Randy said.

"I didn't think business attire would be appropriate, so….." she pointed to her jeans and sneakers, smiling.

Wanting to get right to work, he cut short the small talk. "Let's get to it," he said walking away.

Marie was surprised at his attitude. What had changed? She followed behind feeling like a chastised child. She opened her iPad to the blueprints and positioned herself accordingly. She noted Randy had gone in a different direction. Ignoring his signal to follow him, she continued in the other direction. As she walked she heard, ***"This is not right."*** Stopping short she gazed around, had he heard it?

"Marie! Marie!" Randy said as he ran towards her. The look on his face told her what she needed to know. "We need to go, now!" he said breathlessly.

"Randy, what the heck is wrong?" Marie asked.

"We just need to go, this place is all wrong. I'm sure if we go back to the office we'll find confirmation in the blueprints,"

"Fine, let's go," she said as he practically pushed her towards his car.

By the time they got to the car Randy had regained control over his emotions, feeling a bit silly at his reaction he said, "Sorry, I didn't mean to rush you. It's just, well, you know....." he babbled on as they sat in the car.

"Randy, stop. Take a breath. It's okay," Marie said, feeling sorry for him. Evidentially he had never heard Spirit before.

"I'm fine!" he said, sounding angry.

Marie sat back and let him drive. They exchanged no further conversation until they arrived at the office. Randy parked the car and did not attempt to get out.

"Randy, I heard it too," Marie whispered.

He turned to face her, looking shocked, "Were they, dead people, you know from Katrina. I think this might be haunted," he said seriously.

Marie couldn't help giggling, which made Randy mad, "What's so funny? Do you think I'm crazy? You heard it too, what did you hear?"

Marie managed to get control of the conversation. She explained it wasn't haunted, that was a falsehood. Spirits make themselves known to those that are open to them. What we need to do is find out why this site is wrong.

"Spirit?" Randy asked, wondering if this had anything to do with what his mother told him.

She looked at him, smiled, and said, "We have a lot to discuss, but first the blueprints. Are you ready?"

Marie felt a little out of place dressed in jeans. But quickly put that aside as Randy rolled out the more detailed blueprints on the drafting table. Looking at the big picture, Marie and Randy saw it at once. Why hadn't the drafters picked up on it? Ecologically the building would impede the protected wetlands. Since Katrina, new laws have been in effect to protect areas from flooding. Including buildings in lowlands.

"Randy, you need to bring this before your board. They can't build here. If you like I can ask my boss if we can find another site," Marie said.

"You're right, let me make a phone call. I think we are probably done for today. I'm sorry," he said.

"Right, done here. But not done with us," Marie said, pointing to him, then herself.

"Let my driver take you to pick up your rental car. Maybe later, dinner?" he asked.

"That sounds fine, call me," she said, as she headed out of the office.

CHAPTER FIFTEEN

Marie

Marie's day at the office ended earlier than she expected. She picked up her rental car and headed for Flo's condo. After finding a parking space she decided to walk to Jackson Square.

The weather was turning, clouds rolled in and Marie felt sprinkles. Ignoring the rain she walked through the square towards Cafe du Monde. Deep in thought, she didn't feel the rain until it was pouring. She ran towards the closest building with an overhang. Three other people were seeking shelter under the covering at the same time. A man and two teenage girls.

"How long will this last?" one of the girls asked.

"I have no idea, but in Charleston, where I'm from, they don't last long," Marie answered.

"Charleston? Wow, I have a friend from Charleston. Small world," he laughed.

Marie was stunned, that laugh, she knew it. Suddenly things started to make sense. "Really, well it's a big city, lots of people," she said as she dashed out into the rain. She couldn't get back to the condo fast enough.

Taking off her wet jacket, Marie threw it on the dryer as she stripped off the rest of her wet clothes. Walking into the kitchen Leona and Flo looked at her but said nothing. They had become experts in observation. It turns out that sometimes you learn more from being silent.

"Geez, what a day! First Spirit shows up at the job site, then Randy hears her, then I think I met Lenny, then I get soaked...." she babbled on.

Flo had enough, "Stop! Blessed be, take a breath,"

Marie stopped short, "I'm so sorry, it's just that so many things happened today."

Leona suggested that Marie go take a shower while they prepared lunch. Then they could continue their conversation.

Marie headed to her bedroom with all intentions to shower. As she stripped off the rest of her wet clothes and slipped on her bathrobe; she spotted the small makeup case. She sat on the edge of the bed and opened the case. Taking out all her toiletries she found what she was looking for.

The letter was yellowed from time and folded twice over. She gently opened it. As she read it she cried. Cried for all the lives that had been cheated out of love. The love of a wife and the love of a father.

By the time Marie got in the shower, she was mentally exhausted. I can't take anymore today Spirit, please have mercy, she thought. Mother Earth's lifeblood washed over her as new energy was infused. She loved how water gave her clarity. Marie took her time dressing; what she had to tell Nana and Auntie Flo was too important to rush.

The smell of soup drifted into her room making her hungry. Marie picked up the letter and a few pictures, tucked them into her pocket, and headed to the kitchen. The table was set with bowls of soup, and a large loaf of french bread and butter sat in the middle. Three tall glasses of IPA beer rounded out lunch.

"That was a long shower, we thought you might have taken a nap," Flo said smiling.

Leona felt it, good news from bad….the fairies. Seeing the look on Marie's face she asked, "What is it, child?"

Marie handed Leona the pictures, "I found these."

Leona looked at them, not realizing at first, "Where? Who? Oh, my Goddess!" She looked at Marie and then at the pictures, "It's Ronald and your mother. You look just like her!" As she passed the picture to Flo, she said. "I never met her…."

"Nana, you haven't seen these before?" Marie asked.

"No, where did you get them?"

"The attic, when I went to get a suitcase, there was a makeup case sitting right there. I thought it would be good for my toiletries. These were inside," she replied.

"To be honest, I haven't been in that attic since the workman put all of Ronnie and Patrice's belongings up there. It was right after they died," Leona said sadly.

"There's more?" Flo said.

"Yes," Marie handed Leona the yellowed letter.

Leona looked at the letter, afraid to open it, "It's alright sister, Spirit allowed it," Flo said.

It was a confession to a lover,

Fatu, My love, they have taken you from me. I've tried so many times to find you. They block me every time. There have been times I didn't want to go on. All our dreams are gone. It was one of these times that I strayed, I cheated. I swore I wouldn't have another but it happened. A year after you were gone there was a party, I got drunk. The girl was so kind to me, she listened to our story. She assured me that one day it would be set right. She laughed and spoke of generations to come. I was under a spell, probably the alcohol. I slept with her, imagining it was you one last time. I'm so sorry, it meant nothing. You and only you are my only love.

Your loving, Ronald

Leona was crying, and when she looked up, so was Marie. She passed the letter to Flo, who read it twice. Flo looked at them both and smiled, she knew. But Leona had to come to her own conclusion. By the look in Marie's eyes, Flo knew Marie understood.

"My son loved your mother very much. I wished I would have known. How incredibly sad," she muttered.

"Nana, he didn't even know I existed. My mother's family made some horrible mistakes," Marie said, reaching for Leona's hand.

"Yes, they did," she whispered. Then like a bolt she jumped up! "Oh, my Goddess! Do you know what this means!" Leona was shouting, as she looked at Flo and Marie.

CHAPTER SIXTEEN

Cecilia

She knew the call was coming, she felt it. All was about to be revealed, just as Spirit told her years ago. She sat in her library counting her blessings. Looking back, her life could have gone smoother. But then she wouldn't have the love of her life. Richard Fiord fell in love with her, baggage and all. It didn't matter to him that she was what they called back in Charleston, damaged goods. A label that took a long time to fade from her mind. They built their life on honesty, he knew all her secrets. He even welcomed Spirit, who eventually helped him cross over. She was a very wealthy woman who devoted herself to educating young girls. Cecilia wanted all girls to know they had choices; learning the right ones was hard. Life was one choice after another.

The phone rang, and she answered. Yes, of course, she'd come. She was on autopilot, trying not to think about her story. It had to be told, for Leonard's sake. Cecilia showered and dressed. Slipping on her heels, she found her favorite hat and gloves. Cecilia Renard Fiord was no one's damaged goods!

Her driver dropped her off at Flo's condo. She took a deep breath and rang the bell.

The door opened and her friend Geraldine hugged her, "Come in, you look wonderful,"

"Thank you, it was so kind of your mother to invite me to lunch," Cecilia said nervously.

They walked into the kitchen where Flo, Leona, and Marie sat. They all exchanged pleasantries and a bit of small talk before Flo pulled out the bottle of bourbon. Cecilia smiled, they had done this once before. She started to relax as she sipped her drink.

"Cecilia, you asked us to help with Lenny. We have some information that might help," Marie said.

"I have something I'd like you to read, please," Leona said, handing Cecilia the yellowed letter.

The room was silent as she read, tears rolled down her cheeks before she said a word. " Yes, it was me. I wasn't a hundred percent sure until I read this. No one else knew about our conversation," she looked at Leona, "Lenny is your grandson."

"His laugh, it's Ronald. That's why I thought it familiar….. oh Marie," Leona said, "You have a brother!!"

The room erupted in tears and laughter, each person telling their version of a family tree with many branches. Leona added a new grandson, Marie got a brother, and Cecilia was welcomed into their fold. Ronald had given them all a gift, one that would go on for generations.

With all the celebrating, Marie suddenly said, "Who's going to tell Lenny?"

CHAPTER SEVENTEEN

Lenny

Lenny liked Grace, she was down to earth and pulled no punches. He called her a few days after their initial meeting. Knowing he had a few weeks off, he figured maybe he could help in some way. She welcomed his assistance and invited him to lunch that day. They met at an outdoor cafe just east of the city. Grace liked to give her business to the locals who lived where she was rehabbing.

"Good to see you again. I was surprised you called. What happened to the few weeks of relaxing," Grace said smiling.

"Well, you can only do so much relaxing by yourself," he laughed.

They found a table near an old magnolia shade tree and ordered sweet tea. Lenny dove right in with questions about Mahalia's Place. He was intrigued that someone could take such a personal interest in an area she had no memory of. Many years before Grace had been involved in an accident, leaving her with permanent amnesia. Never knowing she had left a grandmother waiting and praying for her return every day. Mahalia was Grace's grandmother; when Katrina hit, Mahalia refused to leave for fear Grace would return.

She died there waiting, it was the house's spirit that reached out to Leona. Grace started Mahalias Place in honor of her grandmother.

As Grace reminded him of her story she saw a dark aura around him. Being sensitive to Spirit she knew there was more to him than met the eye. He needs to work, she thought. Too many memories follow him. He needs a distraction.

"I realize you have a job, but if you're willing, I'd love to get your opinion on a few renovations I'm doing."

"Actually, I took a leave of absence from my job," he said. Grace looked at him questionably but said nothing. "I know you'll think I'm crazy but I feel drawn to your project, figured I'd give it a try," he said, holding his breath for her response.

"Wow, that's a big decision. I welcome your help. I'm not sure I can pay you what you're worth though," Grace replied.

"Grace, I don't need the money. Truly, right now I just need to feel like I'm making a difference."

They ordered lunch and sat for the next hour discussing different projects Grace had in mind for Lenny. He told her of his experience and his love of getting his hands dirty. To him, building something was a birthing process. It was at that moment that he realized he had substituted buildings in place of a child. The child he and Jade had wanted. If he couldn't create a baby, then he would create something that would live forever, a building. The realization took him by surprise. Being with Grace was good for him, he thought. I'm glad I called her.

Lenny grabbed a trolley and headed back into the city. For the first time in years, his heart felt lighter. Jumping off at Jackson Square he decided to grab a coffee at Cafe du Monde.

Standing in line he realized the girl two spots up looked familiar. She got her coffee, turned, saw him, and smiled. Yes, he knew her, from where?

Finding a table wasn't hard in the middle of the day. He sat facing the square and sipped his coffee.

"Is this seat taken?"

It was that girl, "No. Please sit," he said looking at her strangely, "Do I know you?"

"Yes, we got stuck in the rainstorm the other day. My name is Marie."

"I remember now, I thought you looked familiar. You're from Charleston, right?" Lenny asked.

"Wow, you have a good memory, yes, I am," Marie said while sipping her coffee. She couldn't believe that Spirit had thrown them together like this. It wasn't supposed to be her, they had decided that Cecilia should be the one to break the news. Marie had to think fast, she decided to text Leona, tell her she was here with Lenny, and ask for help.

Marie's cell phone beeped, "Sorry, do you mind? It's my Nana texting," she said.

"Go right ahead, please."

Leona's text message wasn't much help, "Follow Spirits lead, all will be well"

Marie thought for a moment, looked to the sky, and said out loud, "I'm in your hands dear Spirit, give me the words….. Lenny, would you like to take a walk?"

Marie and Lenny walked for two hours. Stopping every so often to sit on a bench. The story was unbelievable. But it did answer some questions he had growing up. His heart broke for his mother, who endured the life of an unwed mom. Especially coming from a prominent family.

He questioned Marie about their father, what was he like? Did he look like him? It was then that Marie told him about his laugh, the laugh that started this quest.

"I still can't believe that I am related to those two crazy old ladies!" Lenny laughed.

"You better not let Auntie Flo hear you say that," she giggled, "Why don't we head back, do you need time to absorb this, or....."

"Are you kidding, no way I'm letting my sister out of my sight! We're going to my Mom's house, I need to give her a big hug! Then we're going to collect those crazy old ladies and celebrate as a family! Are you in?" Lenny said excitedly.

"I'm in, brother! Let's go make some memories," Marie laughed.

Grabbing her hand, they jumped on the St Charles Street trolly and headed to the Garden District.

CHAPTER EIGHTEEN

Randy

Randy went over the blueprints ten times. How could they have missed this? It was so obvious now that he knew it was there. It was a good thing that they hadn't started pulling the permits. He would have to find a new site, which would take weeks. This would put the project back months.

Randy wished he had called Marie the other night, but he chickened out. She would be able to find a new site through Sarah. But now he felt funny about calling her. This Spirit thing had gotten to him. It wasn't bad enough that he was drawn to her romantically but now they were connected spiritually. This did not make for a good working relationship.

The company jet was fueled up and ready to go back to New Haven, Connecticut. Randy called his driver and told him to hold the jet. He was going to get some answers.

The jet touched down in pouring rain, great, he thought, it wasn't dreary enough dealing with spirits. He had the company car waiting to take him home, funny, it didn't feel like home anymore. He let himself in with his key and headed for the kitchen.

"Randy! What a surprise, why didn't you call?" his mother asked

"Mother, good to see you," he said as he hugged her, "I have questions, can we talk?"

"You're so serious, is something wrong? Should I call your father?"

"No, just you. You need to tell me what you meant the last time I spoke to you about fairies?" He couldn't believe he was asking her this absurd question.

She looked at him wide-eyed, raised an eyebrow, and smiled. "Let's sit, son." She pointed to the chairs in the library, took his elbow, and walked to a large black leather sofa. It was time the boy knew her connection to Spirit. His mother took his hand and started talking; she felt good telling him about her history. A history that had been awakened in him. Her grandmother saw the fairies and heard their warnings. They came before the good news. But, there were times when the good news brought heartache first.

"Mother, why haven't you ever told me this?" Randy asked.

"My mother had the sight, it scared me. I blamed her for our lifestyle growing up. Typical teenage attitude, it wasn't until I had my child that my sight awakened in me."

Mother and son spent the next few hours talking. Randy started to understand more and saw his mother in a new way. They had finally made the maternal connection he always craved but never had.

"Son, remember, in order for the light to rise up, the darkness needs to be cleared. But know that once you clear that darkness, the light wins. The light always wins," she explained as she sat back feeling exhausted.

Randy knew now what he must do. The flight back to New Orleans the next evening seemed too long. He had his answers, now to act on them. As the jet landed at Louis Armstrong Airport his phone beeped. A text message from Marie that had been sent hours ago made him smile, "You can't run forever…lol It's been days and I've been busy. I have news, call me." It was late and he knew she would be asleep by now. I'll call in the morning, he thought.

The alarm went off way too early. I just went to bed, he thought. Randy got up, showered, dressed, and headed to the nearest coffee shop before going to the office. He wondered if Marie was up yet. I'll call her as soon as I get to the office, he thought. The walk was cool and the coffee helped wake him up. The breeze off the river called him. Taking a slightly different route, he walked up Conti Street until he could see the ripples on the water. They looked different today, shimmering. He stood mesmerized for a moment before a trolly broke his concentration. The spell was broken and he walked onto the office.

Marie sat at the six-foot-long table with blueprints in front of her. He watched her from the glass partition. She was deep in thought, tracing something with her finger. He waited until she looked up, almost sensing his presence.

"Good morning," he said.

"Yes, yes it is. You don't answer text messages?" Marie said sarcastically.

Wow, she wasn't wasting any time. "I was in the air. I didn't get back until late last night."

"In the air, where did you go? I mean we're not finished here are we?" Marie said with sadness in her eyes.

Randy almost felt this was a double question, was she talking about work or their relationship? Women could be so evasive, why didn't they just say what they wanted to?

"No, we're not done, at all! Now, what's your news?"

Looking relieved Marie said, "Since you never contacted me on the next step I decided to do some work on my own. It seems that there's a very large parcel of land that I think could be used for your project. It's owned by the state now and they have no plans for development. Your company could pick it up for pennies on the dollar," she said looking smug.

"Really? Have you actually seen the sight?" Randy said smiling.

"No, it's pretty remote right now. The roads leading up to it are overgrown. But the best part is that it's on a tributary to the Mississippi! And from aerial photos, I could see there's a dock. I'm sure that would need work but it's an asset." Marie said, looking questionably at him.

"Yes, you're right. Good work," he said smiling at her, "When can we see it?"

"If it's alright with you and you've got hiking boots, we have permits to do a walkabout. I didn't want to pull survey permits until I knew what the area looked like."

Marie and Randy sat for the next few hours with the civil engineer going over the logistics of the plan. They decided that tomorrow afternoon they'd visit the site.

CHAPTER NINETEEN

Leona

Leona loved the early morning hours, just before sunup. It seemed nothing existed but her and Mother Earth. She would sit and listen to the rustling of the leaves as the wind blew off the river.

It spoke to her, calmed her, and assured her that all was well. These were the moments she missed her veranda back in Charleston. There was no smell of Carolina Jasmine here or of the sweet magnolias as they bloomed. But her sister, Flo, was here and that was what was important to her now. They had gone so many years without each other. She wasn't going to waste any more time, especially now. Suddenly noticing the sun had been up for some time now, Leona realized that she had been sitting there for hours.

Flo quietly sat down beside Leona, "Good morning sister. I see you are communing with Mother Earth."

"She's wonderful, you know. Just listen," Leona said. The sisters sat for a few minutes as if in prayer. Leona turned to Flo, "I think it's time for Geraldine to teach Marie."

"Leona, it's a new moon tonight! Today would be perfect. I'll call Geraldine. She can come for dinner. But we better make sure Marie won't be out with that handsome guy she claims is her co-worker," they both laughed.

"I'll text Marie, she's at work already," Leona said.

"Leona, how are you?" Flo asked with concern on her face.

"Well, today's a good day I think. I can tell my body is changing. It takes more effort to do things lately," she smiled and squeezed Flo's hand.

Flo knew Leona's time here was limited. They had found each other this lifetime, they would find each other again. She would cherish what time they had left.

Geraldine was more than happy to come to dinner. She loved talking to anyone who would listen about Grandmother Moon. She gathered her teaching materials, rune stones, and crystals to help Marie understand her heritage.

Marie got Leona's text message early enough that she hadn't already made any plans. Tonight was important to her Nana and she wouldn't disappoint her. Marie looked forward to learning more and Geraldine was the perfect one to teach her. Three generations of women would gather tonight, there was sure to be some kind of magic!

Flo cooked her famous jambalaya while Leona puttered around the kitchen. Both women looked forward to the evening.

Geraldine was the first to arrive, a loaf of French bread and other goodies filled her arms. Leona took the bread as Flo rescued a bag that was falling out of Geraldine's arm. Hugging both ladies, she turned her attention to Leona.

"Aunt Leona, how are you feeling? You look well."

Smiling she replied, "Every day our Divine Source gives me is a blessing. I am looking forward to your teaching tonight, I think Marie is ready."

"I agree, she's already experiencing Spirit. I believe her awakening started a few years ago, she just didn't know how to handle it," Geraldine replied. She tore off the end of the French bread and laughed, "I can't help it, I have to eat it."

Marie came home with two bottles of wine. "I tried to find Carolina Sweet Wine, but they don't sell it here," she laughed and hugged the three ladies. They made their way into the kitchen and sat down. The smell from the pot was intoxicating as Flo filled their bowls. Leona tore off a piece of bread and passed the loaf to Marie. She tore off a piece and passed it on as tradition taught them.

Flo sat and recited her prayer of gratitude. "We are grateful for the bounty Mother Earth has given us. And we are thankful for the extended family the Divine Source has blessed us with, Blessed Be."

The ladies enjoyed a dinner of bonding and laughter. They all felt the importance of this night. Each new generation that could carry on their beliefs was a blessing.

Geraldine dove right in. "Just a bit of anatomy first," she giggled, "We are seventy percent water and just as the tides are affected by the phases of the moon, so are we. If you ever talked to a nurse or police officer, they will tell you how full moons affect people. We must learn to embrace these phases. There is an ebb and flow that not only occurs in tides but also in us."

"Tonight is the new moon, in this phase we put forth our intentions for the coming weeks. It is an invitation to start fresh and call in positive energy. You can journal your intentions or make them your mantra for the next few weeks. I use this mantra: I am open to receiving more abundance in my life," Geraldine reached for Marie's hand. "Do you have any questions so far?"

"No, I'm just soaking it all in right now, please go on," Marie replied.

Geraldine spoke for the next hour. She showed Marie runes of the phases and how to identify them. As she spoke, Marie felt as if she knew this, it had just been forgotten. It was then that Geraldine told Marie about their tradition of the crescent moon necklace.

"It is our tradition that each new generation of sisters receives a silver crescent moon necklace. The necklace will be passed on to your daughter when her time comes," Geraldine said.

"If they are passed down, where will mine come from?" Marie asked.

Leona stood up and walked over to Marie, "Granddaughter, you will have mine. You are my heir," she removed her necklace and put it on Marie, "Wear it well, child, it has powerful magic."

"Oh, Nana!" Marie stood and embraced Leona as they both cried, "You need this, especially now," Marie said sadly.

"No, child. It is your time, it has given me many years of magic. The Divine Feminine has perfect timing, we don't question her," Leona said looking toward Flo.

"Geraldine got my necklace years ago. It's tradition, Marie," Flo said, as Geraldine showed Marie hers.

The ladies embraced and thanked the Goddesses for bringing them together. As they sat talking and laughing, Marie couldn't get Randy out of her thoughts. Could Grandmother Moon be telling her something?

CHAPTER TWENTY

Randy

Randy grabbed the new pair of boots he acquired from the sporting goods store last night and put them in a backpack. He was no stranger to hiking, but that was back home, not on the bayou. The young man at the store had suggested the backpack, some insect repellent, and an ax when he heard about the area they were going into. Marie had said it was overgrown, but he wasn't sure how bad.

His driver was picking up Marie at one o'clock so he had plenty of time to look over the aerial maps again. From what he could tell he would have to leave the car about a mile from the actual site. He wondered if it would have been easier going in by boat. But after checking out the dock from google maps it didn't look healthy. Years of being battered by storm winds had made it unusable.

Then something caught his eye, it was two buildings. One smaller than the other. They were completely covered in kudzu, an invasive but beautiful green vine. Strange, no one mentioned a house on that land. It had to be over one hundred and fifty years old. According to state land management, the last known owner died with no heirs. He died about eighteen sixty-four fighting in the civil war. The property has been in the hands of the state since then, most likely forgotten. He wondered if Marie was aware of these buildings.

Marie packed a blanket, a pair of sneakers, water, energy bars, a flashlight, and matches. Leona looked on questionably, "Just where are you going, child? That doesn't look like hiking equipment."

"Nana, you taught me to be prepared," Marie replied smiling.

"Child, you're prepared for a hurricane!" Leona laughed.

Marie looked down at the backpack and laughed, "You're right, old habits are hard to break. Every time I've packed this bag was when we had to evacuate Charleston."

The doorbell rang, it was the driver for Marie. There was no time to rearrange her backpack. Marie grabbed her jacket and pack, kissed Leona, and dashed out the door. The driver held the door open for her as she jumped in.

"Good afternoon George," Marie said.

"Nice to see you, Miss Mary. You and Mr. Randy be careful out there today. That bayou holds spirits that sometimes don't like to be found," George said very seriously in his cajun accent. He always referred to Marie as Mary; she wanted to correct him until Randy explained they were the same name to the bayou people.

"Thank you, George, are you not going with us?" She had assumed he would be waiting in the car for them.

"No, Mr. Randy is taking the Jeep. He thought he could get deeper into the property."

The ride to Randy's office only took ten minutes. They arrived to find Randy sitting in the Jeep. He was looking at an aerial picture of the project site and comparing it to a road map. Seeing them pull up he waved. Marie gathered her backpack as George opened the door.

"You remember what I told you now girl. If them spirits come calling you go the other way," George whispered very seriously.

Marie nodded and smiled, "I will, thank you, George."

"Good afternoon, Are you ready for an adventure?" Randy yelled from the Jeep.

Marie looked at George, he winked and turned away. "Yes, I'm ready if you are."

Randy threw her backpack in the back seat and jumped in the front. He carefully maneuvered the Jeep into traffic. They drove for fifteen minutes before the traffic thinned out a bit. Marie didn't want to break his concentration so she kept quiet.

"The open road calls," he joked. "I love getting out of the city," Randy said as he took the exit off the highway onto a less-traveled side road.

"It is beautiful, in a different way. The Spanish moss gives the trees an eerie look,"

"From the map, it looks like it's going to get spookier, there's a lot of overgrowths."

"How much further?" Marie asked.

"My guess, about fifteen more minutes. From this point on there's not much civilization."

They ended up driving twenty minutes when the GPS announced they were at the coordinates on the map. Randy found a spot off the dirt road and parked. He noted the coordinates once again and jotted them down in a notebook. He took a compass out of his pocket and checked his directions.

"Someone was a Boy Scout way back when," Marie laughed. "You do know that your phone has a compass on it, don't you?"

"Yes, I know that but, if my battery dies or we don't get reception.... hence, my good old compass," he said looking smug.

"Good thinking, I'll give you that one," she laughed.

They put on their backpacks and headed down the dirt road. It was in fact overgrown and had numerous cypress trees that had fallen onto its path. Carefully they made their way deeper into the mangled growth of wild magnolias, thorny blackberry bushes, and yucca plants. Marie was grateful that Randy thought of gloves for both of them. As he led the way he'd hold back the thicker vines until she walked ahead of him. There was no conversation, the ground was too uneven and they needed to pay attention to each step. They came to a clearing and Randy stopped.

"This might be a good spot to rest a bit. Did you bring water? I have some if you need it."

Marie looked around, what a strange spot to have a clearing she thought, "I have a few bottles, thanks."

She took out her bottle and drank. Then an uncomfortable thought dawned on her. What if I have to pee? Crap, there's no bathroom out here. All of a sudden it struck her as funny and she started giggling. Randy looked at her strangely, which made her laugh even harder.

"What the heck is so funny?" He asked.

Marie explained and they both started laughing, "I promise not to look if you don't," Randy said.

"It's not you, I'm worried about. It's some snake crawling into my jeans that scares me."

"Speaking of snakes," Randy pointed to one hanging from a branch.

"Geez, that was right on cue. Please don't talk about wild boar," Marie said, sidestepping the branch.

"According to my coordinates, we should be arriving at the bluff above the river in a few minutes."

Five minutes later they arrived at an area where they could see the river. Looking at the map, Randy suggested walking along the bluff for a bit. He knew the house was in there somewhere but he couldn't see it. He hadn't told Marie about the buildings, he wanted to surprise her. As they walked the overgrowth got easier to get through. It was then that Marie tripped and fell.

She went down hard and her right knee struck a huge rock. Hearing her scream, Randy turned around to find her on the ground.

"Oh my goodness, Marie, are you alright? Wait don't move, I'll help you,"

Marie put her hand on the ground to balance herself when she realized the rock was flat. Looking down she gasped and blacked out. Randy caught her just as her head hit the stone. He laid her down and wet a bandanna with some water. Dabbing her forehead he called her name, trying to get a reaction. He got none, so he checked her pulse. It was rapid and her eyelids were fluttering as if she was having a bad dream. As he dabbed her forehead once again he noticed the rock. Pushing the debris away on the slab he saw a name, Savannah. This wasn't a rock, it was a headstone. His heart skipped a beat, Savannah. He knew that name. He checked his cell phone and sure enough, there were no bars. As if things couldn't get worse he heard a huge thunderclap in the distance.

He checked his map again and decided that the house was only a few hundred feet ahead. Carefully lifting her in his arms he walked towards the house. It seemed to appear out of nowhere, one minute not there, another minute, there. He felt the first raindrop as he kicked open the door. Carefully laying Marie down on an old stuffed sofa he tried to awaken her again.

"Marie, please wake up," he whispered but got no response. Looking around, he noted what was there and what he had to work with. The sky was growing dark and soon the rain would come down harder. He prayed that there weren't any big leaks in the roof.

He emptied his backpack on the floor, then Marie's. He found her matches and a flashlight. And she teased him about being a Boy Scout. He smiled as he quietly thanked her. Collecting wood that had been laying on the porch he lit a fire just as the skies opened up. He covered her with the blanket he found in her pack, checked her pulse again, and noticed a big blue bruise on her forehead. Sitting on an old wooden rocking chair he stared at her. What am I going to do, he thought.

Feeling certain she had a concussion. He went over the treatment in his head from his Boy Scout days. First, keep the patient awake, well that's not going to happen. Second, rest, no activity. I got that covered, he thought. He couldn't remember how long it was okay for someone to be unconscious. He was starting to get worried. It had been a good thirty minutes now. He checked his watch, it was four-thirty. They should have hiked back to the Jeep by now. He realized as long as it continued to rain and she remained unconscious, there was nothing he could do.

Eating an energy bar he started exploring the old house. It had been beautiful once, he could tell by the woodwork. There were numerous pieces of furniture scattered about. Faded out floor to ceiling drapes hung on the window, most had moth-eaten holes. He found a beautiful old sideboard once used as a buffet serving area. Randy opened the drawers, he found a full set of silverware in one and beautiful lace tablecloths in another. Surprised that these items weren't pilfered, he continued to open drawers. He found a package wrapped in what looked like old wallpaper tied with a ribbon. It was the size of a book and he wondered if he should open it.

Randy heard a moan, grabbed the package, and rushed back to Marie. She was still unconscious but sporadically moaning. After making sure she was warm, he settled back into the rocker. He moved it closer to the fire for light and opened the package. It was a diary.

CHAPTER TWENTY-ONE

Savannah Lamprey's Diary, 1850

Randy ran his fingers over the cover to wipe away the dust. He gazed at it mesmerized. There was something about it that was familiar, had he seen this before? Opening the diary, he found beautifully handwritten pages and scrolled in perfect penmanship. He began to read. As each page unfolded Randy became more and more engrossed, forgetting his surroundings, completely immersed in the story. Suddenly he realized someone was standing next to him. Looking up he saw her. She was beautiful, wearing a green gown with ribbons to match in her dark brown hair. He was so stunned that he couldn't move.

She leaned over and whispered in his ear, "You look tired, why don't you let me show you my life," she held out her hand to him. "Come with me." He gazed over at Marie. "Don't worry, she'll be fine. She has others watching over her," she whispered again.

He reached for her hand and the present faded into the background.

It was one of those days you would try to forget, but couldn't. One day your life is happy and the next, well, it's not your life anymore. Savannah was preparing for her 18 birthday when her world collapsed.

"When will my parents be returning?" She asked Beulah, her mammy.

"Lord child, you ask me that every day, they will get here when they get here," she said over her shoulder as she left the room.

Savannah had a bad feeling, she couldn't put her finger on it, a Knowing. Her parents had been away on what her father called business and her Momma called pleasure. It was unusual for them to be away from home this long.

Momma had promised it would only be a few days, it was now over a week. She was anxious for them to come home, after all, there was a ball to plan. It will be glorious, everyone in town will be there. She imagined herself coming down the staircase, the banister wrapped in white magnolia flowers, the smell of them filling the air. Her new gown, deep emerald green to match her eyes, would fit perfectly around her tiny waist. Daddy had insisted that she wear Grandmama's emerald earrings and matching necklace. No one will look prettier, she thought. This ball was her entrance into society, which would lead to her marrying a wealthy landowner.

The days were long and hot, but there was always a breeze. Biloxi, Mississippi sat on the Gulf of Mexico. Savannah's home was modest, considered small by comparison to the other plantation houses. There was a large veranda that wrapped around the front of the house, the ceiling was painted a sky blue as tradition required. Large hurricane shutters surrounded the bay windows and rocking chairs dotted the porch. The rear porch was smaller and overlooked a pond. It had been well-stocked by the caretaker, who could be seen with a fishing pole over his shoulder most days.

Savannah's mother favored the back veranda. She would say "I don't want to appear waiting for visitors if they come calling, they should be announced." Savannah thought her mother was very proper.

The interior was decorated tastefully, according to their status. There were four rooms off the entry hall, a study for her father, with walls filled with law books of all sorts. A music room for her mother was in the rear. There was a piano that no one played, but in polite society, it was a must to have one. The dining room and a receiving room for guests were in the front. The furniture had been passed down from Daddy's family, but Momma did add some pieces from the finest wood tradesman in south Mississippi. The kitchen was in a separate building for fear of fire as were most grand homes of the time. There was a sweeping staircase to the second floor where the bedrooms were. Savannah loved making an entrance coming down the stairs. The servants were housed in quarters in another building, unseen by the family or friends. Her father was a solicitor in town and knew just about everyone around. He especially used to like to tell her mother and anyone else who would listen that he knew all the dirty secrets of the townspeople.

Savannah had no patience. After asking Beulah yet again about her parents returning, a carriage stopped in front of their house. A tall stately dressed stranger got out and approached the door. Before he could get to the porch, Beulah was out the door.

"Can I help you, sir? The gentleman of the house is out," she drawled.

"Madam, I am Mr. Lamprey's business partner. I have some bad news for Savannah, may I come in?" he requested.

Savannah was on her way down to the parlor when she heard the stranger. "Let him in, Mammy. Pray, what news does he have?"

"There's been an accident."

"Oh hell no, no, no." then Savannah fainted.

When she awoke, Beulah and Mr. Taylor were standing over her.

"Oh child, my poor child," Beulah wailed.

Mr. Taylor didn't know what to say, after all, he wasn't used to women fainting around him.

"What can I do?" he asked.

"Fetch some of Mr.'s brandy," she told him sternly, "bring it here."

Glad to be doing something he quickly found the bottle and brought two glasses. He knew Savannah needed a glass, but for him to tell her the rest of the story he needed a glass also.

Savannah's parents were dead. They had been killed in a carriage accident, something about a spooked horse and rattlesnake. It happened a few days ago but the news hadn't reached Mr. Taylor until today. He had made all the arrangements to bring their bodies home. Savannah didn't want to know that part, it was too grim for her to handle. But that wasn't the worst part. Since she was going to be 18 next month and the only heir, Mr. Taylor had to give her the last will of her parents. Those dark ugly secrets her father used to brag about were fixing to come out. It seemed her family had one of their own.

Savannah was adopted, but that wasn't the end...her real mother was her aunt, her mother's sister, Bonita. They had no idea who her father was. Apparently, she got herself in the family way with no husband. Savannah's mama couldn't have children, so they took Savannah in as a new babe, not even a week old. Savannah's mother never talked of her family and she never asked, it just wasn't discussed.

"Mr. Taylor," Savannah said cautiously "Do you know where my real mother is?"

"I do, but it might not be a good idea for you to contact her. Your parents didn't want you to know," he continued. "She's of a much lower class than you," he whispered.

She stared at him, almost angry. "Well, if they didn't want me to know, why put it in the will?"

Mr. Taylor stammered, "Your birth mother stipulated it," gulping. "Just for a case like this, that they died suddenly," he said, afraid to look at her.

So she thought it was ok to keep it a secret while they were alive and could answer questions. But once they were gone and unable to tell her what she wanted to know, she was out of luck for answers. She imagined her Momma was too proper to admit her sister had a bastard, and she raised it, Savannah thought. Suddenly she was angry, very angry.

Mr. Taylor took care of all the things that needed to be done. The funeral was a grand affair, as far as funerals go. Her parents were well respected and feared in the town. Savannah received all the high-bred families coming to pay their respects. They came and went noting how she never moved from her chair. Beulah would bring them into the receiving room. She would shake their hands, occasionally there was a hug, but she showed no emotion. Most townspeople felt guilty that they were a tad happy he was gone, after all, their secrets died with him. What they didn't know was her dirty little secret that played over and over in her mind. Let this be over, she thought. I have places to go,

I need to find my mother. Somehow she knew she would, there was that knowing again.

"Savannah, my dear, your father's debts have amounted to a large amount. He seemed to live above his means. I cautioned him over the years, but your mother always wanted a higher status," he continued. "I am sorry child, but you will have to sell the house and its contents to pay them off. You might have a small inheritance leftover," Mr. Taylor explained.

Savannah felt like the rug had been pulled out from under her, literally. She would have to leave her beloved home, no party, no making a grand entrance down the staircase, and no wealthy landowner to be her husband.

The Lampreys had an addendum to their will that stated once Savannah was eighteen Beulah would get a small stipend and be retired to wherever she wanted to go. She had been loyal to Savannah since she was a baby, sometimes she even thought of her as her own daughter.

"I can't bear to leave you, child," Beulah hugged her as she helped Savannah pack up the rest of her belongings.

"I know mammy, I love you but I have to find my way, things are different for us now," she said sadly, blinking back tears.

She couldn't afford to keep the house. After her father's debts were paid there was just enough for her to live on modesty until she could find a rich husband. But first, she would find her birth mother!!

"Miss Savannah, I found a couple going to New Orleans next month, they offered to share their carriage with you." Mr. Taylor said. "They knew your Mamma and wanted to help."

"If you think it's safe, that would be fine" Savannah accepted.

The house sold quickly; there was always an up-and-coming generation of cotton growers' children that needed a home. Luckily Mr. Taylor negotiated the contents into the sale which wrapped everything up in one final sale. Savannah went room to room, touching, remembering all the items, trying to imprint them on her memory. The shock had finally worn off when she knew the house was no longer her home.

While cleaning out her mother's armoire, Savannah found an old monogrammed pine box she had never seen before. Taking it over to her Momma's bed, she sat comfortably against the headboard propped with pillows. She took a deep breath and she ran her fingers over the top, the letters spelled a word in a different language, "Guerisseuse." Slowly she opened the top, almost afraid of what she would find, she held her breath. There were three pictures on the top, underneath them were what appeared to be dried herbs or flowers, and a necklace with a charm of the crescent moon.

The pictures were faded and one was torn in half. In the first picture, she saw three young girls in strange dresses with the same necklaces around their necks, sitting under a huge tree. The girls all looked alike and two of them were smiling while the third looked mad. The second picture which had been torn in half had two girls, one that was smiling and the other that looked mad, the other smiling girl was missing. They were dressed in pinafores and standing in front of a magnolia tree, the girls had the moon necklaces on. The third picture was of an old woman, dressed like she had seen the gypsies dress in town. She also wore a moon necklace. Savannah was confused, could one of these girls be her real mother? Could the other be her Grand-mamma? Who was the third girl? What was the meaning of the dried flowers?

Too many questions, with no answers. She decided to put the necklace on, when a strange feeling came over her as she knew this was attached to her mother's memory. Now she knew she had to find her mother, she needed answers!

The following weeks went quickly, Savannah helped Beulah get settled at her sister's farm after they packed up what personal belongings they each had. Before she knew it she was on her way to New Orleans and a whole new life. Savannah's carriage ride wasn't pleasant, she had to share the ride with an elderly couple.

Mr. and Mrs. Baldeguard introduced themselves, "We knew your mother well, child, she loved you as you were her own," she continued. "We knew the family history, too bad, too bad," she said sadly. "They had some wickedness bred in them, your mother said."

"What gives you the right to say such things? My mother never discussed our family!!!" Savannah said angrily.

"I am sorry, I thought you knew, please accept my sincere apology," begged Mrs. Baldeguard. Savannah refused to speak for the rest of the trip. How dare she, probably one of those low-class families, she thought. Then remembered what Mr. Taylor had said about her mother being of a lower class.

After following the explicit directions Mr. Taylor had given Savannah and the Baldeguard's driver, she arrived at a small hospital just outside of New Orleans. She had calmed down enough to thank the Baldeguards for their assistance as they left her on the steps of the building.

Sister Mary's Home for Women read the sign. Feeling excited and intimidated at the same time she thought, oh lord, what if she doesn't want to see me or maybe she's dead ...her thoughts were going in all different directions when a young woman approached her standing there.

"May I help you, Miss."

"Yes," she said, "I am Savannah Lamprey. I think your director was expecting me, my solicitor sent word I was coming."

"Yes madam, please follow me, the director will see you out back." She was taken to a large wrap-around porch around the back of the building.

"Welcome Miss Lamprey, please come sit," said a kindly older woman. "I am the director here, my name is Miss Nelson. Alice, please bring us some sweet tea. This porch gets such a beautiful breeze, I prefer it to the stuffy office. You came to see Bonita?" She asked.

"Yes, I believe that is my mother's name. Although I don't know the last name she goes by, my solicitor only gave me this information," she said.

"Your mother is known to us as Bonita Guerisseuse," she replied.

Savannah tried not to react to the news, there was a connection between the box and her mother! Miss Nelson did prove to be as kind as she looked. She made sure Savannah had a place to stay the night and food to eat.

"I'm sure you would like to freshen up and have something to eat before meeting your mother. Alice will show you to your room, then please join me back here in an hour for refreshments," she said smiling.

"Yes, Thank you for your kindness," she said following Alice.

Her room was on the second floor overlooking a beautiful green pasture. Like most of the countryside, it was dotted with magnolia trees. Staring out the window she had a vague memory of a magnolia tree, was it from the picture or a memory of her own? After freshening up, Savannah made her way back down the staircase to the back porch where Mrs. Nelson waited for her.

She made herself comfortable in one of the old rockers next to Mrs. Nelson, Alice brought out a tray of finger food and drinks. They ate in silence, each in their thoughts. When they were done eating, Mrs. Nelson broke the silence, she nodded at Savannah as if to say 'are you ready and told some of Bonita's story.

"Like many French families along the coast they all had stories that came with them from generations past," she said. "Bonita and her sister were raised by their Grandmama because their parents died on the boat immigrating here from France. There were many family members already here along with their Grandmama to welcome them. The girls, although sisters, had different personalities." said Miss Nelson.

"Your mother, Lucie, who raised you was a bit of a social butterfly, a snob of sorts, sorry but true," she said. "She was looking for a husband by the time she was 16. Bonita was a free spirit. She followed your grandmama everywhere, wanting to learn the old ways, and she did. Your mother, Lucie, was the oldest. She didn't like the old ways, didn't like being connected to them. As soon as she set her bonnet on your father they were married and off to Biloxi," Miss Nelson took a sip of her sweet tea and continued.

"Bonita followed the old ways, practiced healing, and had a great talent for herb potions. She was well thought of in New Orleans. She stayed with your Grandmama and took care of her until she passed. Sometime after she died, Bonita moved out to the bayou and tended the sick there. It was a few years later that Bonita found herself in the family way," she paused to think for a minute.

Savannah couldn't contain herself, "Do you know who my father was?" she asked.

Miss Nelson smiled and went on to finish her story, "No, no one knew who your father was. Bonita would never say, only that he was her one true soulmate who died before she gave birth to you. They were married but she never took his name. After she gave up the baby to her sister, Bonita wandered from town to town, never really settling down, never marrying. She dedicated her life to healing the unfortunate, in the small outback villages that had no healer," she said with a hint of admiration.

"About two years ago she came here to us. At first, she worked with the other women, tending to them spiritually, she had a great gift. She taught them herbal potions and spiritual ways of the phases of the moon. It was a few months ago we noticed her mind was going, she would forget things or repeat them. Gradually it got worse, most of her past she had forgotten. I don't know if you will be able to get through to her child, but you are most welcome to visit with her. I can have Alice bring her out here if you like," she said.

"Oh please, just to look into her eyes would be enough for me," she whispered. Savannah sat staring out at the field, any minute now she would see her, any minute now she would know....was I wanted or just an unfortunate bastard? Was this soulmate someone imagined or real?

"Savannah, I would like you to meet Bonita," Miss Nelson said smiling.

As Savannah stood to greet her mother her knees got weak, oh my god....it was like looking into a mirror.

"I knew you would find me, child," Bonita said with a smile.

Miss Nelson quietly slipped away and it was just the two of them. Savannah fell into her mother's arms and cried.

"Now, now daughter, it's ok, mama's here. I won't let anything happen to you," she cooed as if to a small child or babe. They settled into the chairs and held hands for a while, neither one wanted to break the spell.

"You were wanted," stated Bonita as if reading her mind. "Your father was my one true soulmate. We made you so we could forever be together with the Divine after this lifetime," she said quietly.

"I don't understand mother, who was this soulmate and Divine? It makes no sense...." asked Savannah, thinking that Bonita's mind had gone again. Bonita stared off into the distance.

"Were you taught nothing of our heritage?" she asked.

"I just know we came from France a long time ago, that's all. My mother never talked of her family. I assumed they were all dead," replied Savannah.

A sad and mournful look came over her mother's face. "So much lost, so little time, thank you Spirit for bringing her to me," she mumbled prayerfully.

Although her mother looked tired and worn, she insisted on telling Savannah their family history that had been passed down from generation to generation.

"Many years ago The Divine created us, you and me, all of us. The Divine also created a soulmate for each of us. When it was our time to come to earth as spiritual beings, The Divine let us pick the time and place. Although once we got there we forgot all the wonderful things about living with The Divine. But one thing we would not forget was our soulmate, we would have a Knowing. Sometimes it takes many lifetimes to find each other, other times you are both destined to repeat lifetimes together.

The key to forever being with The Divine is to add to the Tree of Life with your soulmate...bring on another generation and pass the heritage onto them" She was looking more tired at this point, but she continued almost as if her life depended on it.

"Would you like to rest a moment, mother?" Savannah asked.

"No child, it must be said, for I don't have much time. You must find your soulmate, have a child, and add to The Tree of Life, this is our teaching. You have my spirit in your bloodline. Know that your father and I will now live as spirits with The Divine forever! With no children, you will repeat another lifetime here, another timeframe, another era. I am only sorry that there is no time for me to pass on our healing ways to you. For you have the ability in you, it's the knowledge you lack." She blurted it all out so fast Savannah almost couldn't keep up, but was afraid to break the spell by asking questions but had to.

"Mother, I found a box, it has pictures in it, would you like to see it?"

"A pine box, did it have Guerisseuse engraved on it?"

Surprised at her answer, Savannah could only nod.

"Please, let me see it."

Savannah ran back up the stairs to her room and got the box. When she returned her mother was rocking back and forth mumbling some kind of prayer or was it an incantation? She handed the box to her carefully. A broad smile came across her mother's face and her eyes seemed to light up.

"She kept it, she promised she would."

"Please Mother, what does it mean, who are those people? asked Savannah.

Bonita sat back and thought to herself, now she must tell all. She went on to explain that when Bonita gave her sister the baby, she also gave her the box. It was to be given to the child on her eighteenth birthday with the story of their family. But now that her Momma was dead it would be up to Bonita to explain.

"The name on the box is my Daddy's family name, he brought that box from France."

" The pictures, who are they? And the flowers?" Savannah questioned.

"I see you never learned patience, my child," she said smiling. She went on to tell her, "There were three sisters on the boat with our parents who died. The picture of all three girls was taken in France before coming here. They were Lucie, your Momma, who was the one frowning, me, and our other sister Jeanne." She saw the shocked look on Savannah's face.

"I have never told anyone about Jeanne, it is very sad. When we got off the boat there was such a crowd. We were separated. Our Grand-mamma found Lucie and me, but we never found Jeanne. We think another family found her and thought she was their relation, so many adults died on that boat," she finished with tears in her eyes.

"The second picture was taken at Grandmama's house in New Orleans, just Lucie and I. She's still frowning, she was never happy after our Momma died. Momma had promised her a new life of wealth and happiness which never happened. She tore that picture, she hated that we were so different."

Bonita needed time to think, rest, and gather her thoughts. She suggested taking a walk, out in the pasture, to stretch their legs a bit. Savannah agreed, even though there were more answers to be had. They walked quietly, Bonita held her hand as if she were a child crossing the street. Savannah found comfort in the gesture. They found a beautiful magnolia tree and sat down under it. Savannah thought, how fitting this is.

"My Grand-mamma was a wonderful and special lady, she was a healer. She took Lucie and me in, loved us, and taught us. That picture of the old woman was of her. Lucie never liked her, she was a Gypsy to her. She wanted to be part of society, not a healer," she paused thinking,

"When Lucie left, she left for a stable, wealthy, normal life, so she thought. After your real father died suddenly and I was alone with no stable home, it was Lucie that offered to raise you. I knew that was the only way you would get a chance to grow up and achieve your dreams, dreams I couldn't give you."

"Oh Momma, I would have been happy with you. I always knew there was a part of me missing," Savannah moaned.

"I know, child, we can say that now, but you don't understand what it was like back then. I gave you a family to be loved," she smiled. "As for the necklace, we are healers that live by the phases of the moon, that necklace was mine. The dried herbs in the box were seeds brought from France that were healing plants, Grand-mamma saved those in memory of my mother. She gave them to me and when I knew I had to give you up, I gave that box to your mother for you."

As she paused she started to nod off, Savannah suggested that they head back to her room. Bonita agreed, and they walked back arm in arm. She settled her Momma into her bed and knelt beside her, kissed her forehead, and said I love you. Bonita told her to wait, this is a blessing handed down from our people for you, remember it and tell your loved ones, "Good Night, God Bless You, Pleasant Dreams, and I Love You". Then she slept, very soundly as if the weight of her sins were forgiven. That was the last time she saw her mother, she passed away that night

Diary, Reed Renard

He hated this place!! Living in New Orleans, working the barges up and down the river since he was 15 became boring. Every day brought the same things with meager pay. He should be grateful he had a company shack to call home if you could call it that. It consisted of a pallet on the floor with two thin blankets. There was a small heat stove just big enough to warm the shack on cool nights or heat a pot of beans. He wanted action, there was more to life than this he thought. He knew one thing, when he saved enough he would leave this place, maybe go north where it's a might cooler. Louisiana summers were so oppressively hot.

"Stop your daydreaming, Reed, and toss those dice," an angry barge worker yelled. Playing dice and cards was their only form of recreation on the barge.

"Yeah, yeah," he said under his breath as he rolled a winner.

"You have some dumb luck, kid, maybe we need to find some big fish in town to play with," another worker laughed.

Reed seemed to have a knack for gambling, when it came to cards he was even better. He found he could read people's expressions and count cards which gave him an advantage. The idea of getting into a card game in town felt good to Reed, I'm good he thought. I beat the heck out of those dumb barge workers, I can surely beat some dumb hick. The next layover the barge had, he headed into town. At first Reed's luck panned out, he won some, lost some. Each time the barge came to a city he found a game. After playing in small local back rooms, he was invited to play at a social club.

One night after doing fairly well he was approached, "Your good kid, but I can make you even better," bragged a gentleman in a dark velvet waistcoat, looking pretty dapper.

Wondering what he had in mind Reed responded casually, "I'm not quite sure what you mean sir, why don't we talk about that over a drink."

Travis taught him well, so well that within a year he had his own dark velvet waistcoat and had quit working the barges. They went from social club to social club around southern Louisiana. After all, you couldn't stay in one place too long if you were cheating at cards, that could get you shot. As luck would have it they found a group of very wealthy landowners who loved to gamble. They were invited to play by a gentleman Travis had become fast friends with, his name was Preston.

Now Preston was a might shady. The thought of someone cheating at cards didn't bother him as long as he was benefiting from it. Reed had been doing well the past few weeks. Fleecing the weak and losing to the strong, just to keep looking legit.

"I know this group has deep pockets," Preston said to Travis one evening, "You think your boy could work some more magic".

Shocked at this, Travis replied, "Sir, I don't know what you're talking about."

"Travis, I know a couple of cheats when I see them. I've been doing this a long time, I want in," replied Preston, "I know more prestigious people who could use losing a few dollars," he said laughing.

Travis and Reed had no choice; they hooked up with Preston, only to find out that he owned the gambling riverboat, The Orleans Belle. He intended to use them to line his own pockets. When Travis found out what his intentions were he wanted out! Unfortunately, Preston didn't see it that way.

"You have two choices, my good man, either work for me or I turn you over to the law," he boldly stated.

" You can't prove anything, Preston, you're just bluffing," Travis said.

"Try me," Preston snarled.

Reed had already made up his mind, he was staying. Working for Preston wasn't so bad. After all, he had nice rooms to live in, plenty of food, and all the suckers to win from. And there were plenty of women to choose from, what could be sweeter? He was rubbing shoulders with society's wealthiest people. Since Reed decided to stay on, Preston told Travis to take a hike. He didn't need to split the money three ways anyway. Reed brought in plenty of dough. Travis tried to talk Reed into going up north with him; there were plenty of suckers up there to fleece. Reed was tired of running, he wasn't going anywhere, he had a good feeling about The Orleans Belle.

Diary, Savannah's New World

It had been two weeks since Bonita passed away. Mrs. Nelson said she thought that she was only waiting for Savannah to find her. In the meantime, Savannah found a room to let until she could decide what to do with her life. She knew she had limited funds to work with. Why is my soul searching, Savannah wondered. All those things her mother had told her confused her even more. Savannah wasn't sure which direction to go in, stay or go. But where she wondered. She was sorry there had not been more time with her mother but grateful that she had found her. What she was most grateful for was the blessing she gave her at the end of her life; it felt as if she had infused her love into Savannah.

While she was leaving a small cafe one morning she bumped into a rather dapper gentleman, "Good morning my lady, please excuse me," he said, tipping his hat.

"Why sir, it was entirely my fault," she said sweetly, realizing he was a man of means.

"Please allow me to buy you an espresso and beignet," he offered, seeing a potential new girl for his business.

"May I introduce myself," bowing he stated, "I am Preston. I haven't seen you here before my dear, are you new to the city?"

"I am, sir," she replied.

They continued their conversation while sipping their very strong espresso. Savannah wasn't going to let this opportunity slip through her fingers.

Looking back Savannah wasn't sure how she got to this point! This wasn't her plan in life, she was meant to marry a rich plantation owner and be a grand lady. Instead, here she was, living and working. God, she hated that word. It left a bad taste in her mouth. Living and working on a riverboat called The Orleans Belle.

"You want me to wear that!" Savannah said disgustedly, "And do what...I won't be one of those girls for anyone, I will starve first."

Preston had to admire her gumption; it's just the attitude he needed around here to shake things up.

"Slow down little missy, no one asking you to do anything you don't want to," said Preston. "Let me explain what I am offering you, then you can stay or go. It makes no difference to me," he went on. "This job is to attract male gamblers to my boat, keep them in booze, and occasionally distract them at the tables. The dress is part of your job, cleavage sells, girl. Now if you're offered more from one of the gentlemen you're entertaining and you consent, there is a suite of rooms below. But know this, I get 50 percent!"

He finished by lighting a huge cigar and looking very smug. Savannah had no intentions of utilizing that suite of rooms and told him so in no uncertain words. She held her head up high, stamped her foot, and walked away. But not before agreeing to take the job... That had been two weeks ago, two long weeks. Preston had offered her a spacious room to live in and all the food and drink she needed in exchange for working at The Orleans Belle. If she was lucky and the house made a profit each night she got a small percentage. She had to learn to smile and bite her tongue. She watched the other girls and learned their ways. For some reason, the men were drawn to her, even with her aloofness and at times outspokenness. One of the girls said it was because she just didn't care. The men thought they could tame her...

"If I were you I would take your hands off my bottom, sir." Savannah spun around and slapped his face.

"You are a randy one, aren't you girl, making me work for it," a smug man said. "I can pay girl...just name it," he continued. "You'll come back for more," he said now laughing, he loved the game.

Savannah stumped off muttering to herself, over my dead body, asshole. Those episodes only made the gentleman want her more! Preston knew she was good for business. He thought, maybe down the road a bit she would give in and then he would be rolling in the dough, they would line up to bed her.

Reed on the other hand was happy as a pig....he had all the drapings of a grand life. He now owned a carriage and two horses. His wardrobe had expanded to quite a few velvet waistcoats, leather boots, and, of course, a top hat. There was no shortage of lovely ladies he could bed. His good looks and personality dripped confidence which seemed to attract the opposite sex like bees to honey. There was one thorn in his side, Savannah. She was a new girl Preston had taken on. Evidentially she blew through her inheritance or something and needed a job. He wasn't quite sure of her story. She was pretty enough, the suckers would be drawn to her and if she was good enough she would make them all money. They just had to find a way to break her heart of ice.

The temperature was turning, thank goodness, the thick humid air was changing to a crisp breeze. Savannah had been standing at the back of the riverboat watching the paddlewheel and how the water gently rolled off it as they rolled down the river, sometimes it was hypnotic, she thought.

"So, are you thinking of grand things in your future," said a strange man.

Turning and putting on her work smile she said, "Why no, sir, I was thinking, when will a handsome man come to rescue me," then giggled like a schoolgirl. The act was easier now, it had been six months and she was comfortable with her new role.

"Would you join me for a drink," he asked.

"I would be delighted sir, I am Savannah," she replied, fluttering her eyelashes, waiting for him to introduce himself, he didn't.

He extended his arm and she took it. They walked up to the next level where the bar salon was located. It was a beautiful room, red velvet drapes with gold tassels adorned the windows. The same covered the tables with flickering candles. Savannah often imagined that this is what her grand home would look like.

After they sat and he got a glass of wine for them both, he introduced himself. "I am Rufus Baudoin madam, I am pleased to finally meet you."

Savannah smiled.

"I have heard that you have several men wrapped around your finger, do you have a special one?" he asked.

"Why sir, how have you heard such things, I only just met you," she said coyly.

"There is talk among the gentlemen, talk that they would like to get to know you better," he said whispering slyly. "If there is a beau in your life I shall leave you alone, I don't need pistols at dawn," he said.

"No Sir, I have no beau, nor do I need one. I am managing just fine, thank you," Savannah knew her clientele, playing dumb to his identity was part of the game. She was aware of his business, he owned a local brothel and was a scoundrel.

"If you're tired of all this, I can make you rich, come work for me," he said.

Savannah let what he said sink in, she wasn't a prude, she understood.

"Rufus, may I call you that," he nodded. "Rufus, may I have a few days to think over your offer, a girl needs time to think," she said, winking.

They finished their wine and Savannah suggested he try his luck at the tables. She knew her job, drawing the suckers to the table. But something was different about him, dangerous, there is no way she was working for him, especially in a brothel. When she got Rufus settled at a table of high rollers, Savannah sought out Preston.

"He did what?" Preston said angrily.

"It was a job offer at a brothel. I think he's stealing your girls right out from under your nose," she replied.

"And your reply?" he asked.

"You have to ask that, after the last six months, don't you know me better? NO!" she stomped her foot, turned, and walked out.

Preston had to smile even though he was mad, her stomping foot attitude told him how sure of herself she was, and he liked that. Savannah knew she had the upper hand as long as she held out not bedding the clients. She managed to stay out of Rufus's way the rest of the evening.

Diary, Reed

Reed had been away the last month, it was a long-deserved time off. He was buying a house and some land that needed tending to. The house was old but the land was located on the river and would feel like home after living on the boat for so long. It was one floor with two bedrooms in the rear, and one large room across the front to be used for eating and receiving guests. The kitchen was located in a separate building, in case of fire. There was also a caretaker's hut on the property. He hired a man and his wife to look after the house and land while he was away. The Johnsons were newly married and needed a place to live; it seemed like a great solution. They would live in the house while he was gone, then move into the hut when he returned. Mr. Johnson had expressed interest in planting the fields; Reed encouraged him to make any improvements that they would like. He would send their compensation via a barge that came up the river once a month.

He was on his way back to The Orleans Belle feeling good about his decision. The house was his escape plan. One day, he knew he couldn't gamble for the rest of his life. On his way up the ramp, he overheard an argument.

"Preston, what the hell is wrong with you? The girl is a goldmine, give her to me and you will see a profit," Rufus was shouting.

"She is not mine to give away, sir....she is a free woman who makes her own decisions," Preston shouted back as he turned and left Rufus standing in front of Reed.

"Tough night pal," Reed said, passing him by.

"I get my way. You don't turn your back on me, Preston, you will pay for this," Rufus stormed off.

After grabbing a drink at the bar Reed found Preston in his office."What the heck was that all about with Rufus?" Reed asked, knowing he was a high roller.

"My God, Reed, he offered Savannah, that new girl, a position at his brothel. She wouldn't give him an answer so he came to me....he actually wanted to buy her!!!" He said as spittle came flying out of his mouth.

"He just disgusts me, I never liked the man, always trying to take our girls away," continued Preston. "Why the girl has never used the suites down below, she's just not that type. She plays her part, but not that far," he was exhausted now.

"Well, I guess I got back just in time," replied Reed as he poured Preston a brandy. "You want me to handle it? It sounded like a threat to me," said Reed.

"No, not just yet, let's see if his threats pan out. Just do me a favor, keep that pearl handle gun close by. Also, while Savannah is on the gambling floor just keep an eye on her for the next few days," asked Preston.

"Sure boss, whatever you say," he said, but was thinking, crap, now I'm a babysitter.

Days went into weeks and things stayed calm on The Orleans Bell. Rufus never came back.

Savannah was glad she never had to give him her decision. She was never aware of the interaction between Preston and Rufus. She was, however, aware of Reed always being around the corner so to speak.

Almost bumping into him one evening she said, "Wow, I thought this boat was a lot bigger, but you seem to be everywhere!! Why haven't I seen you this much before?"

"I guess you just never noticed me, you wound me, madam," he said with a smirk.

"We never really have spoken before sir, you are always at the tables and I am working," Savannah replied.

"I would like to rectify that madam, please join me for a drink in the salon," Reed said, extending his arm.

She was drawn to him. "Why I would be happy to sir," she said, smiling.

Reed led her to a table in the corner, after he ordered two brandies he asked "What exactly brought you to The Orleans Bell, may I ask if it's not too intrusive?"

"My financial situation led me to find gainful employment, sir. Unfortunately, my upbringing didn't prepare me for anything but being a wife, of course, to a wealthy man," she threw her head back and laughed.

He was struck....that laugh, I know it.

"Just look at me now, hardly wife material or wealthy," she said now smiling sadly.

"I am sorry for your unfortunate circumstances madam. The Orleans Bell has benefited from your presence, I especially," he said.

She looked at him strangely, "And how is that, sir?"

He wanted to tell her the truth, that he was drawn to her. That she captivated him. Instead, he said, "Why madam you bring the high rollers to our humble establishment, and that makes us money," he replied smiling. They enjoyed another brandy and continued their conversation, neither wanting to leave.

"It is getting late, time for me and you to go to work, sir. I wouldn't want Preston to think we were slacking off," she giggled.

"As you wish, my dear," he said, kissing her hand as he stood to go.

As she walked away she looked over her shoulder, something was different, why hadn't I noticed it before? There was a knowing, yes, that feeling in her gut. Was this what Bonita was talking about? Could this be her soulmate? She hardly knew him, how could this be, she turned and watched as he rounded the corner out of sight. Savannah remembered her mother's blessing before she passed and silently said, 'Good Night, God Bless You, Pleasant Dreams and I Love You....my love.'

The following day Preston escorted Savannah to an appointment at the dressmaker in New Orleans' French quarter. Her plan was to get fitted for her new dresses and have a luncheon with Preston who was buying his allotment of alcohol for The Orleans Bell. He escorted her to Jeanne's Dress Emporium. She was to meet Preston at a small outdoor cafe only three doors down when she was done. Miss Chloe assured them it would only take two hours, she hated standing still for hours on end while Chloe measured and pinned away. Savannah never had any patience and this time was no different, she squirmed and shifted from one foot to the other until Miss Chloe had enough.

"Madam! If you don't stop moving about we will never finish," she said exasperated.

Savannah took a deep breath, allowing the fitting to proceed with no more fidgeting. Since she was bored, she asked Miss Chloe how long she had owned the shop. Chloe told her she had only been the owner for a short six months.

"Oh, I was told the owner, Jeanne, would be making my new dresses, is she even here?"

"I'm sorry to tell you, the owner passed away six months ago, rather suddenly. I inherited the shop and never changed the name. I am her daughter, Chloe Guerisseuse."

Savannah's mouth fell open, it was then that she noticed the moon necklace. Her Aunt Jeanne survived! She had a cousin, she had a family. At that same moment, all hell broke loose.

After Preston went about the business of ordering the alcohol for The Orleans Bell, he headed for the cafe. The cafe had outdoor seating with wrought iron tables and chairs that sat in the shade of a huge magnolia tree, the smell was intoxicating. He ordered two glasses of wine and waited for Savannah. He was just finishing his glass of wine when Miss Chloe came running down the street.

"Sir, sir, she was screaming. They took her, they took Savannah, came in the back door, just like that, and grabbed her." cried Chloe.

"Slow down woman, you're not making sense, who took her?"

"Two men, ugly smelly men, they grabbed her and said to tell you, Rufus says no one turns their back on him." Chloe had collapsed into a chair fanning herself.

Preston gave her the remaining glass of wine and left. His carriage couldn't go fast enough; he had grown very fond of Savannah. He knew Reed would help, he also knew that Reed had become sweet on the girl.

"Reed, my office now, hurry!" Preston shouted running up the ramp. Reed followed behind knowing something was terribly wrong.

"We have a situation, Savannah was kidnapped by Rufus." he blurted out.

"What? When?" Reed looked shocked, "You were supposed to be with her in town today." he said looking concerned.

Preston was gulping down brandy straight from the bottle while telling him the story. Reed knew exactly where they had taken her; Rufus had a brothel on the outskirts of town. But he couldn't go in guns blazing, he needed a plan. There was a knock at the door.

"Sir, a message just came for you," a waiter said, "Come in, come in"

Rufus had sent Preston a note calling him out. "A duel in the morning, bring your second, be there at dawn. Savannah will be released when you arrive. You impugned my reputation and I want retribution."

Diary, Rufus

Savannah struggled with her kidnappers. She punched and kicked them but they were stronger. Suddenly one of them covered her face with an awful-smelling handkerchief and she struggled no more.

"Did you harm her?", Rufus questioned the men.

"No sir, she fought like a hellcat, we had to chloroform her," replied one of the men.

"Put her over there till she wakes up," Rufus checked that she wasn't harmed and left the room.

Slowly Savannah became aware of her surroundings and remembered what had happened. My god, she thought, would Rufus go this far? This can't be happening... she tried to stand up and got nauseated. Gradually she was able to get to the door, it was locked...that would have been too easy, she thought. She had heard stories of young women being forced into prostitution, her blood ran cold. She sat in the corner with her knees drawn up to her chin, thinking, how am I going to get out of this? I won't give them the satisfaction of seeing me scared, it's a fight they're going to get!

Rufus came back smiling slyly, he had food and wine. "I see you are awake my dear," he said.

Savannah jumped at him, knocked the tray of food out of his hands, and struck him across the face.

"You! How dare you! What the hell were you thinking? You can't keep me, prisoner. I won't be a prostitute for anyone, especially you!" screamed Savannah, lunging at him again. Not expecting her reaction, Rufus tried to gather his wits. Putting his arms up to protect himself he grabbed her arms.

"Calm down woman, you're not a prisoner nor am I in need of another prostitute," he said trying to settle her down.

"What is this then, why?" She pleaded.

"I don't like losing, Savannah. I asked you to work for me. When you sidestepped my request I asked Preston to release you to me," he said.

"What," she screamed again, "I am not someone's property."

"That is precisely what Preston said," Rufus replied. "I would have accepted it if he didn't turn his back on me!! No one does that, you are but a pawn in this fight."

Savannah was speechless, all this over some stupid manly pride. "I demand you release me, your pride is no concern of mine," she said haughtily.

"All in good time, my dear. In the meantime, try and make yourself comfortable, it won't be long," he said with a sinister smile.

Diary, Reeds Memory

Meanwhile, Reed went to his quarters and on the top shelf of his closet he took out a gun. The last time he used this gun changed his life. He quickly flashbacked to younger years... His mother was unwed when he was born. She raised Reed by herself, doing whatever it took to put food in his belly. She would bring home men at times and send Reed out to play; he didn't realize what was happening until the neighborhood kids started teasing him. He continued to pretend that he didn't know what was happening until one night. He came home to find a thug beating his mother.

"Get lost kid, this whore owes me," he said as he kicked her in the ribs.

"Run, Reed, get help," his mother pleaded.

He turned and ran, ran till he couldn't breathe. No one would help them, not in that part of town. He ran into a huge burly dockworker and bounced off.

"Woah there boy, where you headed in such a rush" laughed the man. Reed confessed the whole story to him as he was crying.

"Buck up, are you the man of the house or a boy?" the man asked.

"What can I do? He's a big guy and drunk," replied Reed.

"I have an equalizer. If you promise to run numbers for me I will help you," the man said. Reed was so distraught that he would have promised anything.

Big Jake explained, "I have a gun, it's not loaded, but if you take it and threaten the guy he might leave."

Reed replied, "Hell yeah, I can do that."

As Reed ran back to his house he kept thinking...I'm the man of the house, I can save her. The closer he got the more panicked he was.

"Leave my mother alone!" Reed screamed as he burst through the door.

"You again, kid, anyone ever tell you you're a pest" the man yelled.

Reed raised his arm, and his mother and the man saw the gun at the same time. With horror, his mother cried "No, Reed, no."

The big ugly man laughed, "What you gonna do with that boy, it's nothing but a toy," and reaching to grab the gun it went off. The man fell back and landed on the bed, eyes open and unblinking Reed knew he was dead.

"Oh, my God, Reed, what have you done?" His mother now panicked and yelled.

"It wasn't supposed to be loaded, the man told me," he cried.

"You have to run, you can't stay here, they will put you in jail," his mother said while shaking his shoulders.

"Go, I will find someone to clean this up," she hugged him and turned away. There was only one place he could go, back to the docks.

Snapping back to the present, Reed loaded his pearl handle gun, the gun he swore he would never use again. But he knew he had to get to Savannah, no one else could. It was the gut feeling he had when Preston told him she was taken. The Knowing, why didn't he feel this before....it didn't matter now, all that mattered was getting her back.

Savannah was awakened while it was still dark, told to dress quickly, and ready herself to leave. Rufus's carriage pulled up to the house, he shoved her in and they set off. As the sun rose over the wetlands, Savannah, Rufus and his second stood waiting for Preston. They didn't have to wait long. As the carriage approached the group, Reed jumped out.

"Rufus, there will be no duel this day, Preston has sent his apologies but stands by his response to you, no one owns Savannah."

Rufus's face went red, "This is a further insult, sir! You will represent your employer. As his second, you are bound to duel me," Rufus responded by taking a threatening stance.

Before Reed knew it Rufus went for his gun. Things seemed to go in slow motion from that moment on for Savannah. Rufus aimed but not before Reed had his gun out and fired. The bullet was true, it hit Rufus in the chest. Without even thinking, Reed turned to shoot the second as his gun was ready to fire. But the second grabbed Savannah at that very moment and pulled her in front of him. Again Reed's bullet was true. It hit Savannah in the chest!

"No, no, no." Running to Savannah, Reed was crying, "No!!!" He held her, she was still breathing.

"I am so sorry my sweet, I love you...please don't die," he buried his head in her neck. He couldn't let her die here in the marsh.

Reed gently carried her to the carriage, placed her on the seat, and headed for the boat. "Hang on my love, we will get help," he said all the while knowing it was useless.

They arrived at The Orleans Bell, Reed gathered her once again in his arms and ran for the boat. Preston saw them coming.

"No, not Savannah" he moaned.

They called for bandages and water as Reed placed her on his bed. Preston drew aside one of his men and sent him to get Chloe; he knew she was a healer for the people of the Quarter. She would be their only hope since the closest doctor was over an hour away.

Diary, Chloe

After going back to the shop and cleaning up the mess the men had left, Chloe gathered her herbs and potions for she knew....knew they would come for her. It had been years ago that her mother had told her of her heritage, her power within. She worked alongside her and learned of the Goddesses and herbs but most of all she learned of the moon and the reverence for its phases. With the moon in its dark phase, a time of new beginnings, of rebirth, she would be needed.

The following morning, a man came rushing into the shop yelling breathlessly, "Madam Chloe, please come, there's been a shooting, she's at the Belle, I have a carriage."

Chloe was ready, she grabbed her bag and beat the man out the door to the carriage. Unfortunately, the horse suffered the whip while trying to race to the boat.

Chloe found Savannah lying motionless on the bed, Reed was holding pressure over the site with blood seeping between his fingers. He appeared to be in shock, mumbling something like, we just found each other again. This can't be it, not another lifetime. Preston gently helped Reed to the chair across the room and let Chloe do her work. It seemed like hours that she worked on Savannah. The whole time she remained unconscious, thankfully, as Chloe had to dig deep to remove the bullet. She cleaned and packed the wound with herbs and applied a poultice.

Exhausted, she finally addressed the men, "Honestly, at this point, I don't know if she will survive. The wound will need cleaning and poultice changing twice a day."

"What can we do?" Reed pleaded.

Chloe explained that only time would tell. If she had a strong will and reason to live she would fight, it was now up to Savannah. There was always the danger of infection so she volunteered to stay with Savannah and care for her. She gave the men a list of items she would need for the next few days and sent them away. She needed rest.

Savannah dreamt as she slept. She saw a huge blossoming tree, its limbs hung down with savory fruits begging to be picked. There were people all around the tree laughing and celebrating. There was a beautiful bright full moon in the sky. They encouraged her to join them. Something told her it wasn't her time. She still had to find him, he wasn't here, not realizing who "he" was.

Reed had been coming every few hours to check on Savannah. Chloe made excuses to leave to give them time alone. She knew Reed was encouraging her to live. She had overheard some of his conversations, about not losing another lifetime, completing their journey. Chloe's heritage told her they were soulmates; it would be tragic if Savannah died. She would do everything she could to make sure she lived.

The moaning woke up Chloe. Savannah was feeling the pain, this was good. She bathed her and spoke to her, encouraging her to live. While tending to her, she spoke of her heritage. Since there was no one to talk to, it seemed perfectly natural to be telling Savannah this. Healers tend to be great storytellers. She started at the beginning of what she knew, as her hands cleaned and repacked the wound she explained her family history.

Her mother had come here from France on a boat. Her parents died on the voyage and when they arrived in New Orleans she was separated from her sisters. A family of healers found her wandering in the streets crying, she spoke no English. They took her in and made many attempts at finding her real family to no avail. She learned broken English and the family realized that she had healers' hands. She was taught the traditions with herbs, the moon, and the Goddesses. There was also the tragic death of Chloe's father; she never knew him. Her mother Jeanne took her family name for Chloe, Guerisseuse

Chloe started humming as she worked, straightening the room and making sure a cool breeze came through the windows.

She heard a soft voice, "Her sisters were Bonita and Lucie."

Chloe almost fainted. She turned to face Savannah whose eyes were open as she was attempting a smile through the pain.

"Oh my goddess, how did you know that?" She asked before even inquiring how Savannah felt, bullet hole and all.

Chloe sent word to find Preston and Reed, only to find out that they had been summoned by the constables to appear in the matter of the shooting at the courthouse. The cousins talked for hours. Of course, Chloe did finally inquire about her pain and administered some herbs to help. Savannah told her that after hearing her last name at the dress shop she realized that Jeanne was her aunt. They compared what they knew of the family, filling in the blanks for each other's history. It ended up to be a fulfilling afternoon for both of them, seemingly alone in life.

Reed came barging in when he heard she had regained consciousness. As Savannah had fallen back asleep, exhausted, Chloe quickly updated him on her wound and how it was progressing. Then their discovery of being family. He was just as astonished as they were. Chloe encouraged him to sit with her until she woke up on her own. She needed the rest to heal. Speak softly to her of your love, it will help in the healing. Reed looked at her strangely.

"How did you know," he asked.

"We are a family of healers, we know one another brother," she said, hugging him and then leaving the room.

He did as he was told. Reed held her hand and told her of things to come. The places they would visit, the family they would have, and the cousins their children would share with Chloe. All new dreams he now had.

She was aware of him speaking but couldn't decide if it was a dream or real. She knew that voice, Knew those mannerisms, it was her soulmate, but where was he...she reached for him, somewhere amid her dream and suddenly he was there! Holding her and crying with her, it was Reed!

Preston and Chloe gave them time alone before barging in. If it wasn't so tragic it would be a joyful feeling seeing them all laughing and crying at the same time. Reed helped Savannah sit up in bed with pillows propped up all around her. Preston had broth and beignets brought in for her nourishment while they made sure she was rested enough to talk to each one of them.

After assuring themselves that Savannah was going to survive, the reunion turned into a celebration of sorts; more food and drink were brought in.

Reed and Preston explained what happened at the courthouse, how Rufus's second admitted that Rufus drew first and Reed had only shot in self-defense. The second, however, would be charged for the shooting of Savannah. Reed would be charged a monetary fee for dueling since it had been outlawed years ago. Reed couldn't apologize enough for shooting Savannah. His guilt was overwhelming, even though she knew it wasn't her he aimed at. He couldn't get that moment out of his head.

As Chloe spoke, Preston felt a weird reaction to her. He knew her mother but had never met her, maybe it was just the situation that got him flustered. Preston insisted that Chloe have a suite of rooms to stay in while she helped Savannah heal. He also sent over one of his girls from the boat to assist at the dress shop. Chloe was very grateful.

It had been a long afternoon and now she insisted that Savannah rest. She chased out the men promising they could return in a few hours. She went about cleaning Savannah's wound and reapplying a fresh poultice, then she gave her an elixir for rest. It seemed they both needed rest. As soon as Chloe saw that Savannah was sleeping soundly she also closed her eyes and drifted off.

Chloe was careful with what she allowed Savannah to do; the wound was in an area that could open up easily if she were to lift anything or bend over suddenly.

Savannah was going stir crazy, "I need to get out of this room, can we please walk the deck. I miss the paddlewheel," she begged Chloe.

She agreed with one stipulation, Reed must take her, just in case she tired and needed to be carried back. Savannah thought that she was being a tad dramatic, but agreed, anything to get her out of this room.

Reed arrived bowing to them both, "Your wish, my lady, is my command," he said joyfully, kidding.

Savannah's reaction was anything but joyful, she fainted! Reed and Chloe rushed to her side.

"What the hell?" questioned Reed.

"Savannah, are you ok?" asked Chloe.

She opened her eyes, seeing them both hovering over her. Was it possible to live in two lifetimes at one time, she thought? She had heard him say that to her in another time and another place. Savannah wasn't able to put her thoughts into words so she sidestepped their questions.

"I am so sorry, I guess I overdid it, I'm ok."

They settled her into the chair and brought a brandy to sip on. Her color returned and she seemed fine to all those around her, she knew different. With the walk put on hold for today and Savannah looking better, Reed went back to work. Savannah asked Chloe if she could sit and talk. She needed to tell her what happened, and she would understand.

"It was as if I was in two places at one time. He said that to me before," she told Chloe with an expression like, help me! "Am I going crazy?"

Chloe calmed her down with one word, Knowing, she was experiencing the Knowing. She had indeed known Reed in another lifetime; Chloe explained what she had heard Reed say to her when he thought she wouldn't live. As they talked more, Savannah started to understand all the teachings that her mother had spoken about.

"Just know that you and Reed have another chance, you found each other, and you can add to the tree of life." Chloe went on to explain, "There are more of our teachings that you can learn, do you understand the meaning of the necklace you wear?" she asked.

Savannah fingered the crescent moon charm on the chain, remembering the feeling she got when she put it on. "My mother left it for me, it was hers'."

Chloe took her necklace out from inside her collar, "We share the same roots, our mothers were healers who honored the old rituals."

Savannah looked puzzled, "rituals?" Chloe decided that it had been a long day. There was a lot for Savannah to take in, she needed time to rest.

"Why don't we finish this conversation after we dine? Preston and Reed, have planned a special dinner."

Realizing that she had seen and felt much too much this afternoon, she readily agreed. She was, in fact, suddenly very hungry. After making sure Savannah was strong enough to walk out on the deck, the cousins headed to the back of the boat.

The cool breeze felt good on their faces, and the smell and sound of the water being churned by the wheel felt like home to Savannah. It was where she and Reed talked for the first time. As they rounded the rear of the boat they both let out a gasp...it was the most beautiful sight, a table covered in a red velvet cloth, flickering candles, and champagne glasses. There were three pedestals with bigger candles also flickering in the moonlight, it was magical.

As Reed approached her, Savannah felt the rest of the world melt away. It was only them. Neither one noticed that Preston and Chloe had disappeared. He took her hand and gently pulled her into a soft embrace. They kissed for the first time, here in this lifetime. They both knew they felt it, another journey. The stewards came and served dinner, the wine flowed and they hardly noticed anyone else. The evening was perfect and ended in a surprise. As Reed walked Savannah back to her suite she thought it couldn't be any better. She opened the door to her room and found it filled with flowers, beautiful roses everywhere she looked.

"What have you done, Reed?" she laughed, and when she turned back to him he was on his knee.

"Savannah, my love of many lifetimes, will you marry me?"

She forgot all about her wound and jumped onto his lap which knocked them both to the ground laughing and crying.

"Yes, yes, oh Goddess yes!" Chloe and Preston seemed to appear out of nowhere with a bottle of champagne and glasses.

"Congratulations, you guys!!!" yelled Preston.

Chloe was busy hugging Savannah, "You knew about this," Savannah asked. Chloe just nodded, smiling.

Savannah woke the following morning still feeling wonderful, that was until she tried to move. Her side hurt, when she placed her hand over the bandage she noticed blood. Something had gone wrong, it was not supposed to be bleeding. She made herself get up and rang for Chloe. By the time she arrived Savannah was panicking,

"I'm bleeding Chloe," she said, lifting her hand and showing her.

Quickly getting her back to bed, Chloe rang for Preston and Reed. After taking down the dressing she saw the problem, the wound had burst open.

Chloe ran to her room to gather her healer's bag, the wound didn't look good, she would have to work fast. When she returned to the room Preston was pacing the floor while Reed was kneeling at Savannah's bedside holding her hand.

"I guess I overdid it last night," she said softly.

"I never should have surprised you like that, I think I am to blame for all of this," Reed said. He never anticipated that she would jump into his lap in her excitement, but that's probably what opened the wound.

The men were asked to leave while Chloe tended to the wound. It still bled, this time more stitches would be needed. A new batch of stronger herbs was used in the poultice to draw out any infection. Savannah had taken the pain elixir and was now fading in and out of consciousness; this helped Chloe work deep into the wound. After about an hour she allowed the men to return to Savannah's side. She was in a deep sleep by now, mumbling at times, something they didn't understand.

"Please let her rest, the wound was deeper than I thought and she's lost more blood. I don't want her to move for at least a day or more, let the stitches adhere," Chloe said, exhausted.

"I will stay with her," Reed said. He felt so guilty and it showed on his face.

Preston tried to tell him it was no fault of his, no one could have predicted that Savannah would have reacted the way she did. Chloe suggested that she and Preston leave them be while they cleaned up and had some coffee in the salon.

"I will send a steward with a pot of coffee for you Reed, do you want a beignet also?" she asked.

"No, thank you, coffee is fine, maybe a shot of brandy, too," he replied as if in another world.

A few hours later Chloe looked in on the couple, Savannah was still fast asleep while Reed had laid down on top of the covers next to her and also fallen asleep. She thought it best to leave them be, there was nothing else she could do at this point.

Savannah's moaning woke Reed. He gently wiped her forehead with the herbal soaked cloth. All the time talking to her. Her skin felt like it was on fire. He rang for the steward who went to get Chloe. It didn't take long before both Preston and Chloe appeared. They seemed to be together all the time now. Chloe quickly determined that the fever was bad, she wasn't sure if she could heal her this time. She bathed her body with cool herbal water, applied a new poultice, and waited. Now it was up to Savannah, her will to live.

Chloe encouraged Reed to talk to her. It appeared to Chloe that Savannah was drifting between worlds from the mumbling she could understand.

"Talk to her Reed, she needs grounding in this lifetime. Tell her of your love now, at this moment."

Reed didn't quite understand what she meant by grounding but he did love her and had no problem telling her that. He told her of his house on the bluff, the beautiful view of the river, and the children they could raise there. He told her of the dreams he had that inspired him to buy the house in secret, the dreams that one day he would find her. It seemed that he talked for hours before her eyes finally opened.

"Oh Reed, it sounds so beautiful," she said weakly.

He was crying, he never cried. He wanted to hold her but was afraid he would hurt her. She held out her arms to him, he again laid down carefully next to her.

"Tell me more about this place, I want to go there, it's home," she said strangely.

He told her of the gardens and the deer that ran free through the woods. He told her of the front porch and the rocking chairs they would sit on while they grew old.

Realizing she had fallen back asleep, he shut his eyes from exhaustion and slept. He dreamt of children running on the bluff and chasing each other. He saw Savannah sitting in the rocking chair smiling, then he saw a gravestone. It was overlooking the river, so he was afraid to look at it. When he did, he woke up, never knowing who it was. He was so rattled by the dream that he called for Chloe. She assured him it was only a dream, it was his guilt making its way into his dream state.

But Chloe knew what it meant, these two soulmates would have another journey in another lifetime. Chloe bathed Savannah's sweat from her body, changed her dressings, and again applied a herbal poultice knowing all the while it was senseless. She called Reed back in along with Preston, this time they all stayed. Chloe looked out the window and realized it was a full moon. She and Savannah should be dancing under it, she thought. How cruel that they had all just found each other, only for this lifetime to be taken away. Savannah opened her eyes, she saw nothing but love around her, love she always wanted but was afraid she'd never find.

She gazed up at Reed and said "I will love you forever, I will find you again in another lifetime. Please, Reed, take me home."

The carriage and wagon pulled up to the house on the bluff. Preston, Chloe, and Reed got out. The caretaker's family had arranged everything, it was all prepared for them. Solemnly they had brought Savannah home.

CHAPTER TWENTY-TWO

Randy

Randy closed the diary and sat in stunned silence. Tears were streaming down his cheeks. There was a knowing about this story as if he'd heard it before and forgotten. He glanced over to Marie who seemed to be sleeping more peacefully. Feeling the need to stretch, he walked over to the window. It was still dark but the rain had stopped. Strange how at peace he felt among the chaos. Randy walked from one room to another, touching furniture and doorways. He knew this place, his soul belonged here.

Suddenly feeling exhausted, he headed back to Marie. He added another log and stirred the embers in the fire. Looking at her sleeping so peacefully he felt the need to lie down beside her. Gently he took her in his arms and cradled her head. Exhaustion encompassed him and he fell into a deep sleep.

Was it a dream, was it real? A man was standing on the porch looking out onto the bluff. There was no overgrowth, just magnolias, and bluebells. She would have loved the bluebells he thought. Randy felt the deep sorrow coming from the man, the despair was overwhelming. He tried to awaken himself but went deeper instead.

Randy looked on as if having an out-of-body experience. The man was telling a young woman he had to go, there was nothing left here for him. Her spirit pleaded with him but he turned away. The country was at war, they needed him now more than her. She had been gone for a year now. He lived with her spirit too long. He gazed out at the headstone, Savannah, it's time, my love.

Marie's soft moaning pulled him back, out of the depth of his dream. He kissed her forehead and hushed her back to sleep. But there was no sleep for him. What the heck was that dream, he thought. Once again he gently laid her head back down as he got up, stretched, and realized that it was getting light out.

As he was devising a plan in his head to get them out of there, he heard a whirring sound in the distance. It was coming closer. He ran out onto the porch and saw a helicopter landing in the clearing. As he watched he saw George emerge and run towards the house.

"George! Over here," Randy waved, "How did you know?"

"When you didn't return I knew something was wrong. We sent the local police out last night, they found your Jeep. But by that time, it was dark and storming. I contacted your father and he hired this whirlybird," George said pointing to the helicopter, "It sure is good to see you, sir."

"You have no idea. Marie's hurt, she fell and hit her head yesterday,"

"Where is she? Can she walk?" George asked.

"She's inside, no she's still unconscious. We need to get her help, now!" Randy replied.

Randy and George managed to get Marie safely into the helicopter. As they were lifting off Randy took one last look down and swore he saw a beautiful woman smiling up at him. He blinked twice and she was gone. Something told him he'd be back, for more than just his Jeep!

The helicopter landed at the University Medical Center fifteen minutes later. Marie was rushed into the ER, Randy followed and gave all the information to the attending doctor on duty. They escorted him to a waiting room and a nurse told him she'd update any information as soon as it was available. Meanwhile, Randy made some much-needed phone calls. The first to thank his father, then the one he dreaded the most, Leona.

Leona was napping when Randy called. Flo answered her cell phone. He told her about Marie and their evening, assuring her that the doctors were taking good care of her.

"Flo, my driver is on his way to get you and Leona. I'm so sorry," Randy said, choking up.

"It's not your fault, son, you did everything right, taking good care of our girl. I'll wake up Leona and we'll be there soon," Flo replied.

Randy paced, sat, then paced some more. Time seemed to be standing still. When he checked his watch it had only been thirty minutes since he left Marie, it felt like hours. While he was gazing out the window someone called his name. Turning he saw the young doctor who was caring for Marie.

"Doc, tell me, is she going to be alright? Can I see her?"

"She's awake and asking for you, she's suffered a nasty bump on her head. There is a slight concussion but nothing more."

"Awake! Why was she unconscious for so long?" Randy asked looking relieved.

"I can't answer that question. Let's just say, sometimes our bodies know what we need better than we do. She needed to rest and her body took over. She'll have a full recovery. You can take her home in a few hours if she remains stable," he said, smiling.

Randy thanked him a few times, shook his hand, and followed him into the ER. When he pulled back the curtain surrounding her bed she was sitting up. She took one look at him and burst into tears.

Randy rushed to her side. He gently engulfed her in his arms as she cried. Assured that she wasn't in pain, he allowed her to cry.

"I'm so sorry, I just lost my footing. I've caused you so much trouble. They tell me a helicopter brought me here?" she said questionably.

"Yes, you can thank George for that. He knew we hadn't returned and got concerned. But we'll talk all about that later. I think your Aunt and Nana will be wanting to see you. They should be here by now, I sent my driver for them."

"Can they wait just a minute, there's something I need to tell you. A dream, it was so real…."

Before she could continue Flo and Leona rushed in. There was such a ruckus over Marie that Randy had to step back. They kissed her forehead, then checked all her limbs, as if the doctors missed something. As the mother hens did their thing, Randy took the time to call the office.

His secretary was happy to hear from him but surprised. She thought he'd be taking the day off with Marie being in the hospital. After explaining Marie's updated condition he asked her to research some information.

"I need to know who owned that land before the state assumed it. It's really important so if you have any pull with the public records department I'd appreciate it."

CHAPTER TWENTY-THREE

Marie

Marie was settled onto the couch, and Leona covered her with a blanket as Flo brought herbal tea. It had been a long twenty-four hours. Randy brought her and the ladies home in his company car. Once he knew she was resting comfortably he'd made his excuses and left. He knew Leona had a lot of questions for Marie and was just being polite with him there. He had his own questions to get answers to.

As Marie dozed off she heard Flo and Leona whispering, they seemed to be waiting and watching. She was in the twilight part of a dream when she heard, ***"Don't change my flow."*** Her eyes flew open, and she sat up.

"Marie, what is it?" Leona questioned, seeing her distress.

"Nana, I heard her. She spoke to me," Marie said with a faraway look in her eyes.

A worried look passed across Flo's face as she looked at Leona. "Marie, look at me child, who spoke to you?"

Marie looked at them both, "Is it possible for the river to speak through spirit?"

"Yes, child. Water is one of our precious elements of nature, the fairies live on top of it. You've seen them, haven't you?" Leona said.

"Remember your teachings, water, air, fire, and earth. I like to add spirit, Mother Earth nurtures me as I live in her spirit. She has room for us all," Flo added.

This was not what Leona had imagined her conversation would be this evening. Marie still hadn't talked about her ordeal last night. Spirit had interjected just enough to change the subject. Leona wasn't having it. Excusing herself she went into the kitchen. She had questions that needed answers. She called Geraldine. When she returned to the living room Flo and Marie were deep in conversation. They looked up at her and smiled.

"Come sister, sit," Flo patted the seat next to her, "Our daughter has some news."

"Nana, there's something I need to tell you," Leona sat and nodded for her to go on, "It started last night, a dream. It was as if I lived before, the dream was so real. I only remember bits and pieces. There was a man, I knew him before. I found him, but I died. It's so confusing. There was a big house, one like Randy said he found after I fell. Please tell me what it means?"

"Marie, I called Geraldine. She's coming over," Leona looked at Flo, "She can talk to your Spirits, we'll get the answers."

"Talk to my Spirit?" Marie questioned.

"Geraldine has a gift, she's able to connect with spirits that came before us. Those from another lifetime," Flo answered.

"I'm confused, what does my dream have to do with the water spirit?" Marie asked.

"I don't know, hopefully, Geraldine will help us with that. How about a fresh cup of tea?" Leona asked.

The ladies headed into the kitchen and sat down just as the doorbell rang. Flo went to answer as Leona set out the cups. Geraldine stood at the door with a bag of beignets in one arm and a large loaf of crusty French bread in the other.

"Geraldine! Why didn't you just come in?" Flo asked.

"Sorry mom, but my hands were kind of full," she said holding up her packages.

"Let me help, here give me the bread," Flo said as she tore off the top piece laughing.

"I knew you were going to do that," Geraldine laughed along with her, "Where is everyone?"

"In the kitchen, Leona's making tea."

Before they could close the door a firm hand pushed it back, "Hey, can I come in?"

"Lenny! Of course, come in. Did you hear? I gather," Flo said.

"Yes, from Grace, who heard it from Randy's secretary, of all people!! Why didn't someone call me?" Lenny questioned.

The ladies looked at each other, they weren't used to a man in their group, Geraldine laughed and broke the ice, "You're right Lenny, but things happened so fast. I guess we're not used to Marie having a brother yet," she went over and hugged him, "Come sit."

Before sitting, Lenny made his way to Marie, hugged her, looked at her closely, making sure she was okay, and asked, "What were you guys thinking, hiking out in those woods?"

"Oh Lenny, you're just in time. Geraldine was going to talk to my Spirit…….."

Before she could continue, he said, "I just came by to make sure you're okay. It is too early for spirits. Anyway, Grace has me on a wild goose chase, something about land ownership. Probably a new property she's refurbishing. I'll let you ladies do your thing. I love you, Sis," Lenny said as he kissed Marie's cheek, punched her arm in jest, and said, "Stay out of the woods."

The ladies settled down to tea and beignets. Marie caught Geraldine up on her evening and her dream in between bites. Geraldine just listened, she allowed Marie to talk for as long as she needed. Any interruptions could sidetrack tidbits spirit could be hinting at. Without realizing it Marie revealed more than she thought.

When she finally paused and looked at Geraldine, she said, "Am I crazy?"

"No, Marie. What I believe happened here and Spirit should back me up is……" before Geraldine could go on, Marie interrupted.

"Savannah…..I remember a name!"

Geraldine looked at Marie, "Yes, hopefully, you'll remember more as we go along. As I was saying, I believe Spirit led you to that place. It was no coincidence, remember everything is connected one way or another. Your unusual unconsciousness opened the door to Spirit. It was definitely Spirit-led."

"Aunty, we were on a potential job site. How could that be Spirit-led?" Marie questioned.

"Think about it, why were you at that particular site? What drew you there? Who picked it? All these questions will lead right back to Spirit."

Marie sat for a moment thinking, "You're right! I found the defect in the original site, then I researched new sites!! You mean I was being directed all that time and I didn't know it?"

Geraldine explained, "Yes, Marie, I believe a large part of our decisions are based on spiritual guidance, we're just not aware of it. Think of your intuition or gut feelings, they are guidance, you just call it something different."

"So you're saying, I had a connection to that area in another lifetime?"

"It appears so, you left something unfinished. If I had to guess, I'd say it was love," Geraldine said smiling, as Flo and Leona nodded in agreement.

"Randy, we have a connection. I felt it before. Could he be the man?" Marie asked.

"I don't know, we'll have to talk with him. Do you think he's up to our mumbo jumbo?" Geraldine laughed.

"After last night, yes. He had so many questions," Marie replied, "But Aunty, why did Spirit talk to me today? It wasn't a dream like last night. It was a statement."

"What exactly did Spirit say?"

"Don't change my flow."

Geraldine contemplated for a minute, looked directly at Marie, and said, "It will become clear in the future, but remember what the water spirit said." Geraldine got up, shook her arms and hands out, bent over and touched the floor then smiled.

"Aunty, what was that all about?"

"When working with spirits, sometimes negative ones find an opening and sneak in. You should always shake off any unwanted spirits and ground yourself afterward," Geraldine said.

CHAPTER TWENTY-FOUR

Lenny

Working for Grace had been a blessing for Lenny. He needed something more grounded and found it in these old houses. Sometimes he went days without thinking about Jade, where months ago he couldn't go for hours. Finding a sister was the icing on the cake. Who would have thought? It scared him that just after finding her he could have lost her. I've got to meet this Randy guy, Lenny thought. He suddenly felt responsible for someone else and it made him feel good.

The courthouse was packed. Lenny wondered what was going on. It seemed that the state had given amnesty to people who owed back taxes. But you had to come in person for the write-off.

He waited in line listening to the stories around him. Some people that thought they lost their homes were able to get them back. Others just wanted to sell them and hadn't been able to. When will the aftermath of Katrina end, Lenny thought, it's been decades.

While waiting, Lenny was able to hook up a few people with Mahalia's Place; they loved the idea of their homes being brought back to life. After twenty minutes his number was called. The woman at the counter seemed overwhelmed.

"License and proof of property please," she said without looking up.

"I'm not here for taxes. I need to find the original owner of a property," Lenny said.

"That's public information, sir, you can get in online."

"Your online records don't go back that far. It seems the state has owned it since the 1890s," said Lenny.

"Wow, that would be one big tax bill," she laughed as she looked up at him.

All Lenny could do was stand there. Her laugh, it was musical, and those eyes.

"Sir, are you all right?"

"Oh sorry, yes. I'm fine. Just trying to remember the property number," he said embarrassed at his reaction to her.

As he fumbled with the paperwork to cover his reaction she waited. Then she noticed something familiar.

Not being able to put her finger on it she asked, "Have we met? You look very familiar."

"I work for Mahalia's Place, pulling building permits. Maybe you've seen me here before?"

"Yes, that's probably it. What's the property address? I'll see if I can find it."

Lenny gave her the address and looked at her name tag as she worked her keyboard. Her name was Winnie. Strange, you don't hear that name very often, he thought. And her accent definitely wasn't southern. He was drawn to her.

Suddenly he felt guilty like he was cheating on Jade. But Jade is gone now, she would want me to start over. He argued with himself as he stood there, not realizing that Winnie was holding out a piece of paper for him to sign.

"Oh geez, sorry. I'm trying to do too much at one time, getting my thoughts jumbled. Where do I sign?" Lenny asked.

"Lenny Renard, that's your name right?" Winnie asked.

"Yes….why?"

"Well, Lenny, I think you need to slow down and take a deep breath. You seem overwhelmed," Winnie said with a twinkle in her eye.

"You're right, I do need to slow down. What time is your lunch break?" he said without thinking, shocking himself. "I'm sorry, I'm not usually this forward, that just came out wrong."

Winnie looked at him as if sizing him up, "I don't get a lunch break, I'm part-time." Smiling, she said, "But I do get off at two o'clock if you want to meet for coffee."

Trying not to appear too anxious he said, "Sure, that sounds good. How about right next door, The Cafe?"

Winnie handed him the property information, smiled, and said, "I'll see you there."

CHAPTER TWENTY-FIVE

Randy

Randy's secretary had come through. Her contacts at the courthouse found him exactly what he needed to know. But this knowledge complicated things all the more. He needed time, time to make things right. To do this he had to avoid Marie, she would have too many questions. He asked his secretary to send Marie a dozen pink roses with a note. He apologized for not being there but was called out of town on business. It was half a lie, it was business. But he didn't leave town.

The first order of business was to find a new site for his project. After deciding on two potential sites he took them to the engineering department. One was thrown out immediately for flood issues. The second had great possibilities. Unfortunately, the board of directors wanted the site he and Marie had explored. It was perfect. There was access to the river and they could widen the tributary to allow a deeper channel for their pier.

Randy knew he had to stop the board from acquiring that land. It wasn't meant for industrial use.

"Your contact at the courthouse, can you hook me up with them?" he asked his secretary.

"Yes, but it's not the courthouse. Ever heard of Mahalia's Place?"

"Isn't that the non-profit that's refurbishing abandoned Katrina homes?" Randy asked.

"Yes, Grace is a friend of mine. She's the owner. She has a guy working for her that knows people at the courthouse. I can give you his name if it's ok with Grace," she replied. Randy nodded. "I'll call her right now."

As Randy devised a plan in his head, his secretary knocked, "Come in."

She handed him a piece of paper with a name and phone number, "This is your guy."

"Thank you, you're the best," he said smiling.

"Secretary's Day is coming up," she said, laughing as she left his office.

He looked down at the paper, Lenny Renard.....where had he heard that name before?

Randy was sure he knew it from somewhere but just couldn't place it. He punched in the number and waited for someone to answer. Unfortunately, it went straight to voicemail. Randy left a message with his number and hung up. Before he could turn on his computer the phone rang. Looking down at the number, he saw Lenny's name.

"Hello," Randy said.

"Yes, I'm returning your call. This is Lenny Renard."

"Thank you for getting back to me so quickly, I appreciate it," Randy said.

"I was at the courthouse, I usually turn off my cell there. What can I do for you, Randy?"

Lenny knew exactly who Randy was! This was the guy who almost got my sister killed, he thought. I was just thinking about finding him. This must be a spirit thing, he thought, smiling to himself.

Randy explained his plans to Lenny, who seemed impressed. There would be a few days of work here for sure. He'd have to clear it with Grace.

"Randy, I'm meeting a woman for coffee at The Cafe at two o'clock. She works at the courthouse. I think she would be a big help. Do you think you can join us?" Lenny asked.

"Yes, this is a priority for me. Thank you."

"Okay, see you then," Lenny said and hung up. He called Grace, and after hearing his plans, he cleared his calendar for the next few days. This was going to be fun, he thought. I wonder when Randy will realize who I am.

CHAPTER TWENTY-SIX

Leona

Leona sat in the recliner watching Marie sleep. This situation could have ended badly. She thanked the Goddesses for their intervention. Leona truly felt that they had led George to find the couple that morning. It seemed that there was much more of this story to be uncovered. Who was Savannah and why was she showing herself now? Then there was the crypted message of **"Don't change my flow."** How did that play into the story?

Marie stirred, opened her eyes, and watched Leona deep in thought. "I'm okay, Gram. You should go to bed."

Leona smiled, "You're probably right, I'm just concerned about you."

"Besides a slight headache, I'm fine. I feel like such a fool upsetting you all. The weird thing is I never saw that stone until it was too late like it just popped up out of nowhere."

"I think Savannah was trying to get your attention," Leona said.

"Yeah, well, she certainly did! How about next time you want my attention, Savannah, you be a bit more subtle," Marie said, laughing.

Leona knew then that her granddaughter would be fine. Sudden exhaustion washed over her as if she had been held above the waves holding on for Marie. Now the waves crashed over her as she closed her eyes. Deep sleep overtook her and she never heard Marie or Flo calling her name.

Marie noticed it first. Leona's breathing was erratic. She called Flo who was resting in the next room, "Aunty, she was talking to me one minute and the next I thought she was sleeping. But I noticed her breathing, it's not right."

"Leona, Leona, can you hear me? Wake up sister, please," Flo pleaded, getting no response.

"Should we call 911?" Marie whispered.

"Yes," Flo answered.

By the time the ambulance crew arrived Leona was semiconscious. She was mumbling something incoherently about Savannah. Then suddenly she said, "Naomi, I'm not ready yet." and drifted back to semi-consciousness. Flo and Marie looked at each other surprised.

"Who's Naomi Aunty Flo? I've never heard that name before."

"Child, that's your grandmother's guardian Angel. It's been a long time since I heard her say that name." Flo whispered.

The EMTs stabilized Leona and readied her for transport. Flo grabbed a jacket and followed the crew down the stairs to the waiting ambulance. Her heart was pounding, could this be it? Please, Spirit, I'm not ready to lose my sister. Not now, she prayed.

As the gurney was loaded into the rig a kindly older woman held out her hand to help her up. She smiled and assured Flo it wasn't her time. In the rush to get seated she forgot to thank her. Turning to do so, Flo noticed she wasn't there. As she settled in beside Leona, she remembered seeing the patches on her jacket; it was the same as the other crew members.

Turning to one of the crew, she asked, "Where did the other woman go? I wanted to thank her for helping me."

"Other woman? There's no one besides us."

"But she had on ……," Flo stopped, suddenly realizing that Spirit had sent her a message!

Smiling, she placed her hand on Leona's shoulder and whispered, "It's not time yet, dear sister, rest."

The ambulance pulled into the hospital bay and the doors opened. As the crew rolled the gurney out onto the pavement Leona opened her eyes. Before she could speak they were rolling her down a long white corridor. Strange, she thought… Could this be like when I pass over? A corridor filled with light. But then the sounds of the emergency room suddenly interrupted her thoughts.

"Miss Leona, can you hear me? Squeeze my hand if you can," said a concerned nurse.

"I can hear you, my dear, where am I?"

"You're in the hospital. Your family found you unresponsive and called the ambulance."

"My family…..oh sweet Goddess. Are they here, you must tell them I'm all right. They will be so worried, please…" Leona begged the nurse.

"They are here, ma'am. The doctor will speak to them just as soon as he makes sure you are stable. Now, let's calm down. Take a nice deep breath and tell me your history."

"Well, history? Seems this is my third incarceration," seeing the stunned look on the nurse's face she realized what she had said. Laughing, she continued, "oh my that was a slip of the tongue, incarceration may be the right word. But I meant incarnation, I've seen many lifetimes," Leona said, smiling. Seeing the nurse's expression of disbelief she decided it would be better to get down to business before they admitted her to the psych ward.

Flo sat in the waiting room thumbing through a magazine but not really seeing any of the pages. Her mind was on Leona. What were they doing in there? How long before they come to give her some updates?

Hearing some commotion in the hall she looked up. Lenny and Randy were demanding to see Leona! It didn't register at first. Flo thought, what are they doing here? Then they noticed her sitting in the chair looking confused.

"Flo, what happened? Have you heard anything?" Lenny asked.

"How did you know?" She asked.

"Marie called Lenny. We were together at a meeting so I came along," Randy replied.

Flo felt like she had zoned out for a few minutes. Things had been registering slowly, but now things seemed crystal clear.

"Thank you both for being here. I don't know much. She seemed to open her eyes as they took her out of the ambulance but I didn't have time to ask her anything. The doctor hasn't been out to talk to me yet, so I guess we just wait. Lenny, is Marie okay?"

"Yes, just worried, I assured her we would call as soon as we knew anything. I think I'll go call her to let her know we found you," he said, as he hugged her.

Lenny called Marie and promised to call her back the minute they got any news. He had just found his new family and it seemed that the fates were trying their darndest to separate them again. First, his sister fell and got a concussion, and now his grandmother is in the hospital! He was starting to think it was him, maybe he was bad luck for them.

Randy interrupted his thoughts, "Hey, man, you in there?" He asked, poking Lenny's shoulder.

"Oh sorry, yeah, just thinking."

"I'm going to get Flo some coffee, you want one?"

"Sure, in fact, I'll go with you. I need some fresh air."

Flo sat patiently waiting for Randy and Lenny to return when a doctor appeared in the doorway. Quickly standing up she met him halfway across the room.

"Are you a relative of Miss Leona?" He asked.

"I am her sister, how is she?"

"She's awake and coherent. Although she did have us questioning her sanity for a moment. Something about other lifetimes," he laughed.

Flo wanted to hug the doctor! That comment meant more to her than he would ever know.

"When can I see her?" Flo asked.

"I'll take you to her now. I assume you are aware of her condition?" He asked gently.

"Yes"

"She needs rest, no more stress. She told me of her granddaughter's ordeal. It seemed to take a lot out of her. You must remember she doesn't have the same energy levels," he looked over at Flo and smiled. "I expect you'll have your hands full, she's a feisty one."

Leona was sitting up on the stretcher holding court. A nurse's aide was taking her blood pressure while a lab tech was drawing blood. A nurse was writing something on a computer and all the time Leona carried on three different conversations with each one. She loved the attention.

"Why, dear sister, must I make an appointment to see you?" Flo asked demurely.

Seeing Flo brought tears to Leona's eyes, holding out her arms she cried, "I'm so sorry, I didn't mean to scare you all."

Flo gently embraced her sister, kissing her cheek, "No need for apologies. I'm just happy to see you awake. How are you feeling?"

"Actually, rested. But we have much to discuss," she whispered, then winked.

"I found these gentlemen roaming the halls looking for you, Miss Leona. Is it alright if they come in? Asked one of the nurses.

Lenny and Randy didn't wait for permission. Rushing to her side, they both started asking a hundred questions.

"Whoa, guys, slow down. I'm fine. I'll probably go home tomorrow. They just want to observe me for a bit. Why are you both here?" Leona asked.

Lenny explained how Marie had called him. She knew he would want to know, it was his grandmother after all. He happened to be in a meeting with Randy about a parcel of land for Mahalia's Place. So when Randy heard, he wanted to come also, out of concern for Marie. Leona was starting to think her extended family was growing day by day. What they didn't know was the secret Spirit had whispered to her as she fell under the waves of exhaustion.

CHAPTER TWENTY-SEVEN

Lenny

The past week had been a whirlwind for Lenny, finding a sister and a grandmother, and almost losing them. If it wasn't for Grace and his work at Mahalia's Place he would have gone crazy. On one hand, he was happy to have found family. On the other hand, he felt he didn't belong. They all had this Spirit thing going on, it was nuts. Where do I fit in, he wondered.

Grace had a meeting set up for him this morning. But before meeting her he planned on stopping by the courthouse. His side job was cut short by Leona's illness a few days ago and he had unfinished business with a certain young lady.

Arriving early he climbed the courthouse steps. The lawyers were hurrying past him as he took a moment to watch a laughing tourist couple flag down a pedicab. It had been years since he indulged in a ride through the city. Smiling, he hatched a plan.

The line wasn't too long and before Lenny knew it, there she was, smiling at him.

"Why Mr. Renard, what can I help you with today?" Winnie asked.

"Will you indulge me in a pedicab ride this afternoon? It's my way of apologizing for running out of our meeting."

"As it happens, we are closing at noon today for a computer upgrade. I'll be free after that," she replied while shuffling papers.

"Noon, that would be great. I'd love to take you to lunch also. Oh heck, let's make a day of it!" Lenny said a bit too enthusiastically.

Winnie was smiling and agreed to meet him at noon, while the man behind Lenny in line grumbled something about personal business.

Lenny sat on a cold bench outside the courthouse. The magnolia tree limb hung over just enough to yield him shade. A brief horn blasted a warning to another driver two blocks away. He tried to concentrate on the people milling about. But as noon approached Lenny became more and more nervous. Strange, he thought, it's just a lunch date, why am I feeling like my life depends on it? Suddenly he realized he hadn't thought of Jade in weeks. Sadness and guilt washed over him. That is how Winnie found him sitting on the bench.

Watching him for a moment she saw the sadness and felt it in the pit of her stomach. She wanted to reach out to him, hold him, comfort him. It was at that moment Lenny looked up, straight into her eyes. He felt a knowing, he knew her, in another time.

Winnie felt the same thing, it scared the heck out of her. Quickly recovering herself she said in her sexiest imitation of a southern accent, "Hi stranger. Been waiting long?"

Watching her with her hand on her hip posing, he laughed. "Your accent has a hint of New England twang to it."

"As it should my dear, born and bred in Boston," she stated proudly, jutting her chin out.

"Wow, a bonafide Yankee!" Lenny laughed as he stood up.

Not being able to hold in her laugh anymore, she giggled and threaded her arm through his, "So what is this pedicab thing you're taking me on?"

Lenny looked around the street, saw a bright red bike coming toward them, and waved his arm. Winnie thought it looked like a rickshaw and laughed.

"All aboard, madam," Lenny motioned her on first, then followed.

The driver asked where to and Lenny told him to just give them a tour. Which he did, for the next forty-five minutes. The driver talked so much that Lenny and Winnie had little time to get more acquainted.

By the time the tour was over the couple was more than hungry. They walked a few blocks and shared small talk. Lenny found a cute outdoor cafe nestled a block off the river and they found an empty table. The humidity was low and a cool breeze rolled off the Mississippi. The river had its own sweet smell, not like the saltwater of the oceans or the pluff mud of the Carolinas. It had the smell of cypress, Spanish moss, and a bit of something industrial if you could blend them all.

Lenny took the menu from the waitress and pretended to look it over while he gazed at Winnie. She pretended not to notice.

The waitress smiled, "I'll give you guys a moment." She turned and walked away.

"So, what do you think looks good?" Lenny asked.

"I love shrimp and grits," Winnie replied.

"What? A Yankee who loves grits! I'm shocked."

"Actually, my mom was from South Carolina, so I grew up eating grits, crawfish, and hush puppies," she laughed. "I only moved here last year after losing both my parents to cancer. I had an opportunity to transfer and I took it. I thought a change of scenery would do me good." Winnie felt like she just blurted out her life story with one exception, that one would have to wait until she knew him better.

Their afternoon ended with a stroll along the river. Lenny didn't want it to end but Winnie had another engagement. She periodically helped her neighbor care for her elderly mother and tonight was the day.

"Winnie, I don't want this to end. I know this sounds crazy but I feel like I've known you forever. Your eyes, I've seen them before. My friends say that we can live in multiple timelines, that our soul has a spirit and it lives on. I never understood this until now." He held his breath and waited, waited a lifetime.

Winnie just stared at him not quite knowing how to handle this, then a slight smile crossed her face. She took his hands, lifted them to her lips, and gently kissed them, "Welcome home, my love."

Before he knew it she was in his arms and they were kissing and laughing all at the same time.

"What the heck just happened?" Lenny asked.

"You really really have a lot to learn. Now, I have a call to make. I don't think I'll be able to help my neighbor tonight," she said laughing.

CHAPTER TWENTY-EIGHT

Marie and Randy

After settling Leona in for her nap, Marie made her daily call to Charleston to report on Leona's recovery. In actuality, it had been hard to keep their South Carolina family from being at Leona's side, but after much debate, they agreed to daily updates. Maggie threatened to be on the next flight out of Charleston if she didn't follow the doctor's orders. Dora had sent so many vases of flowers that they could open a shop, then there was the case of Carolina Sweet Wine that Martha sent also. It was almost like the ladies were there in New Orleans with them. Marie could feel their spirits everywhere and so could her Granny; Leona meant the world to Marie, she was her Divine feminine connection to Spirit. She had much to learn but each day brought new insights, trusting her gut intuition was the biggest lesson.

A soft knock at the door brought her back to the present. Her heart already told her who was on the other side of the door. Opening it, smiling she said, "Good morning."

"And good morning to you. I tried to knock quietly in case Leona was resting," Randy said, stepping forward and kissing her cheek.

"She is. Come in." turning and heading for the kitchen she asked. "Coffee?"

"Thanks, that sounds good. How about an update on our girl."

Marie busied herself with making the coffee while telling Randy the latest on Leona's condition. There was good news and bad news, the good news was that with proper rest and less stress she wouldn't experience as many symptoms. The bad news is that they will persist, it's just a matter of time. There was another topic that weighed heavy on both their minds, but neither mentioned it. Like an elephant in the room, it stood in the corner waiting, growing ever impatient.

"I've called my boss in Charleston, she's allowing me to work from here a bit longer. I know my Aunt Flo can care for Granny but I want to be here, just in case." A single tear rolled down her cheek and Randy's resolve broke. He reached for her and she allowed herself to be enveloped in his arms. Marie broke, the tears flowed as her heart felt as if it was torn in two.

"What will I do without her?" She whispered between sobs.

Randy had only known Leona for a short time but he felt her presence and somehow knew her Spirit would never really leave them. "She will always be with you, you are a part of her," he said, wiping away her tears.

As she tilted her head to thank him, her eyes locked on his, the kiss was magical. It was a remembrance, a knowing, it startled both of them. "Randy, I'm sorry, I didn't mean.."

"I did," was all he had to say.

In that instant there was no more awkwardness, they found each other. Not fully understanding this, they both started talking at the same time.

"The rock, Savannah, who was she, and the house, jeez Randy, what's happening?"

"There's more, much more, I feel it..." Randy was cut short.

"Can't a being get some rest around here?" Leona laughed, "It seems there are some questions that need answers to," she said sitting down at the table.

"Oh, Granny, I'm so sorry. We didn't mean to wake you," Marie said holding Leona's hand while Randy looked guilty.

"Oh, no, it wasn't you. The Spirits woke me, they made such a racket I couldn't help but wake up. It seems we have a mystery to solve," her smile was so wide and the brightness in her eyes made you forget she was unwell. Marie knew this was what she needed, a purpose.

What Leona didn't tell anyone is that she had a secret, Spirit spoke to her during her trip to the hospital. She needed to speak to Randy alone, but for now, she'd see what direction Spirit took them.

Flo returned home to find the three of them with papers and maps strewn over the table. "Well, I can see there's no rest for the weary in this house," laughing.

"Sister, I'll have plenty of time to rest in my next life, we have a mystery!"

"This is very true Leona, but we need you around long enough to solve this new quest and if you don't get proper rest......well, we'll have to call Maggie."

Randy wasn't ready to reveal his secret. He needed more time, trying to convince Marie and Leona to slow down their snooping was like trying to stop a freight train going downhill, impossible. Flo and Maggie were the only ones who could get Leona to rest. With each day it got easier, she felt the weariness in her body and allowed herself to rest despite the need to push on.

Leona tried her best to rest, she even set aside two times a day to nap. Try as she might, no sleep came, just her mind running through different scenarios to their mystery. It was during one of these naps that she decided it was time to bring everyone together for a family decision. Her illness had caught them all by surprise. Leona had always been so vibrant and full of life, that it was hard to believe this timeline was concluding. She actually missed her Charleston family; it would be good medicine to see them all.

Flo and Leona were having dinner when she suggested her idea, "Flo, what do you think about a family reunion?"

"Now? Won't that be too much stress for you? You're supposed to be resting not planning a party and I know you, you'll be doing it all," Flo replied looking concerned.

Leona looked at Flo, reached for her hand, and squeezed it. "Spirit would like me to be present at my wake," she said holding her breath, waiting to see Flo's reaction.

"Oh, my Goddess! What a wonderful idea! I love it," Flo said with tears rolling down her cheeks.

For the next hour the ladies made lists of family and friends they wanted to invite. The next problem was to find places for them all to stay, that was a task they'd ask for help with.

Marie continued her work with Randy's company. Finding a new site for Amalgamated became a priority for Randy. The two sites he recommended to the board members were being considered. But they liked the site not offered to them by Randy. It was an abandoned piece of land with water access. The tributary it sat on could be widened and a new pier would bring in more business. Try as he might, Randy couldn't convince them that he'd find another plot, one better, closer to the Mississippi.

"Randy, the company's ready to bid on that parcel of land with the tributary," his boss said, "I expect that you and Marie can pull the permits for the boundaries and set up the blueprints. We'll have to petition the state for the sale also. Seems you have some work ahead of you."

"Yes sir, we've been working on that all ready," Randy replied, knowing what he was working on wasn't exactly what his boss was expecting.

When Randy found Marie in the conference room he gave her the news. He needed to go to the courthouse to pull the permits, leaving her there to start work on the blueprints.

"Randy, there's just something about that land that tells me we can't let it be turned industrial," Marie said while pouring over maps."

"I agree, keep at it," he said pointing to the maps, "Make sure you check the new real estate listings for riverfront industrial properties, we might luck out yet."

Kissing her cheek, he turned and was gone. Marie sat for a minute, closed her eyes, and asked her Creator for wisdom and guidance. There was a gut feeling that she needed to save that land, was it Savannah's spirit pushing her? So many questions, so few answers. She opened her eyes and laughed, that was exactly what Leona would say.

Randy called Lenny as soon as he was out of the building. They had work to do and they had to do it fast. The next call he made was to his Mom. She of all people would understand.

Lenny was standing outside the courthouse waiting for him, briefcase in hand, he smiled. "Winnie and I have been hard at work, it seems we can do this!"

"Really? Why didn't you call me?"

"She wanted to make sure all the paperwork was in order before getting your hopes up. Are you sure this is what you want? It won't be cheap?" Lenny asked.

"Yes, I've never wanted anything more. I've secured the money, that's no problem. I think in the long run that will be the easy part," he said laughing.

"I agree, keeping this from my family will be the hardest thing you'll ever do," Lenny patted Randy's shoulder and said, "Let's do this!"

CHAPTER TWENTY-NINE

Winnie and Lenny

It hadn't been easy picking up and moving to New Orleans. Some days it felt like she moved to a different country. Getting used to the different dialects was the hardest. Working in a courthouse brought in all sorts of people and they all seemed to pronounce words differently. The accents included thick French, creole, deeply southern, and sometimes a mixture of all three. There were times when she had to have a person write down what they wanted. She swore they made words up and they kidded her that it was she that had an accent. But as time wore on she caught onto the different sounds and became able to answer questions without saying "what, or excuse me" too many times.

Losing her parents within six months of each other was hard. What was harder was having no one to share that grief with, being an only child. She had put aside her dating days two years prior when her mom first got sick. Moving back into her childhood home put a slight damper on dating. Then when her dad became ill it was all she could do to keep her full-time job and care for them. In the end, hospice was a lifesaver for her. The nurses and caregivers not only took care of her parents but looked after her also. They made sure she had time to herself and encouraged her to go out, but she always ended up coming back early.

Her mother had the sight, she knew a few months before her diagnosis what was to come. It was then that she started preparing Winnie for the future. They would sit for hours as she brought forth generations of seers. Hundreds of years ago they called them witches. Her family tree had branches dating back to Salem. But a slight difference was that her family intermarried with the indigenous people of the area, causing them to be cast out of their community.

Winnie knew she had the sight at an early age, she was able to discern the good from the bad people with their aura. Her mother taught her about honoring the Divine Feminine and following the elements Mother Earth gave us: air, water, fire, and earth. Her observations were honoring the movements of the moon and the pagan holidays that incorporated that aspect. Her mother was very clear to teach her that we all have different paths to follow, some were drawn to organized religion. But her people took a path less traveled which at times led to being seen as weird or heathen.

Her mother would tell her each morning, "Father Creator, Mother Earth, Grandmother Moon, and Grandfather Sun will be your eternal family child, allow them to surround you. Their guidance will never fail." It became Winnie's mantra as she traveled through those dark months.

The phone ringing brought her back to reality. Seeing the caller ID said Lenny, her heart quickened. "Good morning," she answered.

"Yes, it is! Good morning to you, too." Not waiting for her to answer, he went on, "I think we've done it! Randy and I just came from putting in a bid!"

"That's wonderful, are you sure you've covered all the bases? No one else knows yet?" Winnie asked.

"Pretty sure. But Randy would like you to meet us for lunch if you can, just to play devil's advocate. Of course, I'd like you to come, too," he mumbled the last part.

"That would be fine. Can we meet at the cafe next door to the courthouse? I have an hour off for lunch so that would save time. Say about 12:30?"

They agreed on the time and Winnie hung up. The coffee she had poured fifteen minutes ago on her break was cold now. She had really zoned out there for a while. Thinking of the past didn't pop up much anymore but when it did it engulfed her in grief. Winnie was looking forward to seeing Lenny, he made her soul happy and she needed a little bit of that today.

Winnie decided to do some double-checking on Randy's project. It seemed that he wasn't the only one who was doing background checks. Amalgamated Projects Inc had done a title search recently. Who the heck were they, she wondered. They hadn't shown up before. Printing out what she could, she folded up the papers and shoved them in her purse.

Winnie found both Randy and Lenny sipping coffee at a table outside the cafe. An occasional group of tourists would stop by to read the menu posted on the window which was close to their table. Winnie suggested moving inside where it was quieter and they could talk without the noise of the city. As they did, Randy shot Lenny a look, raised his eyebrows, and cocked his head towards Winnie who was leading the way, as if to say, something's up! A slight nod from Lenny said he agreed.

As the waitress was handing them their menus Lenny blurted out, "Winnie, what's wrong?"

Winnie smiled at the waitress, thanked her for the menu, and ordered her coffee. Looking over the table she could see their concern, leaning forward she whispered, "Who the heck is Amalgamated Projects?

"What? Geez, that's the company we were hired by to find a location for their newest plant. I tried to steer them in another direction." He went on to explain how Marie found the first site for them unbuildable and that's how he found the site on the tributary. They had to think fast. "They have very deep pockets, I can't compete with them," Randy said reluctantly.

"Nothing has been done yet, all they did was a title search and that will show the state owns that land now. It will take time for anything to come back. I'll keep an eye out for any movement at my end but you guys need to find a way to steer them to a different property," Winnie whispered.

Suddenly, Lenny smiled, "I think I might have someone who can help us! Grace has deep connections to New Orleans. Maybe, just maybe, she could research that property and find kin to the original owners. Winnie, how long is that tax amnesty going to last?"

"I believe it ends in two weeks. I can check. If she could find a link, the back taxes, which would be astronomical by now, would be forgiven! And you could make an offer before Amalgamated even knew what was happening."

Excited by the new plan the three drank their coffee and made plans to keep in touch throughout the day for any updates.

Lenny walked Winnie back to her office, guiding her with his hand gently in the small of her back. "How about dinner tonight?" He asked.

"Yes, that sounds great. What time?" Winnie said smiling.

"I'll pick you up right here! I don't want you to get away," he said laughing.

Lenny kissed her cheek and set out for Mahalia's Place. He knew Grace would find a way. She brought forth the best in people and Lenny had faith in her.

A sign on the office door told Lenny that Grace was out at a new renovation. Noting the address, he punched it into his GPS and headed to the car. Driving through Mahalia's neighborhood gave him hope for other communities. If only others had the same passion that Grace did. Pulling up to the house on Colby Lane, Lenny saw Grace on the porch roof.

"What are you doing, woman? You have contractors to do that!" Lenny yelled.

"Hello to you, too, Lenny! Come on up," she said pointing to the window above the porch.

Lenny sidestepped broken steps and garbage on the floor to find the staircase leading upstairs. Testing the treads to make sure they were safe he made his way up. He found Grace sitting on the roof waiting for him, looking right at home among the broken shingles.

"Grace, you never seem to surprise me. You have your work cut out for you here," he said looking around.

Laughing she said, "Did Mahalia bring you here? I was going to call you for help and you showed up. Granny knew I needed you."

Randy filled her in on his predicament while he assessed the surroundings for her. If she was surprised by his request she didn't show it. Researching families was her passion, she would be in her element. In the meantime, Lenny pulled out his pen and clipboard and started sketching the floorplan. This renovation would take more work than usual. It appeared that no one had lived there in a long time, just squatters.

Grace crawled through the window first. Shaking off her bandanna and wiping her brow she smiled. She loved this part, taking something broken and making it new again. The neighbors started calling her the house doctor just for that reason.

"Any chance I can get a look at this property you're so involved in?" She asked.

"Well, to be honest, it's a hike. It's so overgrown. We got Marie out by helicopter when she got hurt. There is a dock, but I'm not sure how safe it is," Lenny replied.

"I have access to a boat. Can you get a map of the place from the river?"

"I'm sure Randy can, he's the engineer," Lenny said, sounding excited.

Grace agreed to start her genealogical search while Lenny worked on getting a river map. They would meet tomorrow afternoon to make plans on visiting the property. When Lenny texted Randy, he responded immediately with a schematic of the tributary access which he forwarded to Grace. Spirit was moving things right along. Lenny continued walking through the house for the next hour, making notes and recommendations to give to Grace.

CHAPTER THIRTY

Randy

Randy found Marie in the conference room again. He worried she was pushing herself too hard after the accident. But he could tell she was bound and determined to find another site for Amalgamated.

"Tell me you have good news," Randy asked.

"I was just going to call you and have you meet me at a site. It's a bit further downriver but I think it's perfect," she smiled.

Before he could answer, Betty, the boss's secretary interrupted them, "Randy, Mr. Holmes wants to see you. He's in his office."

Randy looked over to Marie, she shrugged her shoulders and smiled. "We'll catch up in a few minutes," he said as he followed Betty out the door.

It seemed that Amalgamated Projects Inc. wanted the property on the tributary. Mr. Holmes wanted Randy to make a set of plans to their specs. Looking at the list of their demands Randy was stunned.

"Sir, this will take millions to build! I can draw up a set of plans but it will take weeks, the permits alone, we'll have to jump through hoops!"

Mr. Holmes looked annoyed, "It's what the client wants, they're willing to pay us top dollar. That's the bottom line. Now, can you handle it?" Randy silently nodded as his anger increased. "I'll let the client know that we'll have plans ready in three weeks, is that enough time?" Again Randy just nodded, he knew if he spoke he'd probably get fired.

Marie found him sitting at his desk fuming. Papers were being thrown across the room and mumbling could be heard from the door. She thought she heard a few curse words.

"Randy, are you okay?"

Seeing her calmed him a bit. But as soon as he explained the situation his anger went back up. Grabbing his jacket, then her hand he started out the door.

"Come on, let's go. We have a property to look at."

"But…." Marie attempted.

"No buts, I'm not giving up," he turned and smiled at her, "I'm sorry, I overreacted. I don't like to lose, can you tell?"

"Is what they want to do feasible? I mean a pier as big as you said, wouldn't it make an environmental impact on the ecosystem?" Marie asked innocently.

Randy stopped so fast that Marie bumped into him, "Marie you're a genius!"

He hugged her and kissed her soundly on the lips. She was so surprised that she couldn't say a word. Grabbing her hand again he practically dragged her out of the building.

Once in the street, he stopped, "I've got to call Lenny, he's working on something for me. I'll meet you at my car," he said, handing her the car keys.

Randy punched in Lenny's number. He answered a second later, "What's up buddy? I didn't expect to hear from you today."

"Things have changed, Amalgamated wants the property. My boss is expecting me to have blueprints ready in three weeks. I can't lose this Lenny," Randy said, with a pleading in his voice.

"I'm with Grace now. We're making plans to visit the property by boat since it's a hike to get in there. Do you want to join us?

"Why does she need to see the property? I just need to know if any relatives exist to the original owners."

"Sometimes these old houses have clues to who lived there. She's thinking there might be something she can work with."

Randy thought back to reading the diary, there were clues. Maybe Grace was right.

"Makes sense. Yes, I want to go with you. I might have something Grace needs to see," he said cryptically, "I don't want anyone else to know this. So far our group of three just grew to four."

"Don't worry, Winnie and Grace are good at keeping secrets. Plus they're great at uncovering the information we need!" Lenny assured him. "How's tomorrow at ten? Grace wants to dock at high tide. From the aerial photos that's the best time to access the dock that's still intact."

They agreed to meet at the marina just up the river. As Randy finished his call, Marie pulled up alongside him in the car with the window rolled down and her arm resting on the door.

Laughing, she said, "Looking for a good time, sailor?"

Marie looked good behind the wheel of his car. He thought I should make this permanent. "I sure am, good-looking. Take me away from all this," he said while getting into the passenger seat.

Marie maneuvered the car through the downtown traffic onto St Claude Avenue with ease. Randy sat back and watched the city fade into the countryside. It wasn't long before he recognized the old battlefield site in Chalmette. A short time later Marie slowed and turned right. He started to see the potential Marie saw as he noticed the old abandoned industrial factories leading to a pier on the river. Driving as far toward the river as she safely could, Marie stopped.

Turning to Randy she said, "I never promised you a rose garden, but I guarantee this site will save your clients a boatload of money."

Randy laughed so hard that tears rolled down his cheeks. Marie looked crushed. Seeing her expression, he stopped laughing.

"Honey, I'm sorry, I thought you were making a joke. You know, boatload…." He said pointing to the river.

"Oh, I thought you were thinking this site was a joke." Attempting to smile, she added, "You ready to explore?"

They walked on the gravel road leading to the pier. No words passed between them, each making their own mental notes. Randy assessed the surroundings. Direct availability to the Mississippi was a big plus. The pilings would need some work but minor compared to building a whole new pier. They wandered back toward the deserted buildings. Although they were in bad shape Randy thought their structure looked sound.

Marie was the first to speak, "Well, what do you think?"

"I think you hit a home run. We have something else to offer our clients that will definitely save them money. How good are you at using CAD on the computer?"

"I am more than proficient with CAD Civil 3D. That's the program I use the most, why?" Marie answered.

"I can't draw up two different sets of plans in three weeks. I'll need you to do the preliminaries on one of them, you choose. What do you say?"

"Yes! I can absolutely do that. I've already done most of the preliminaries on this site. If you trust me, I can start doing more in-depth work."

With their plans made, they made one more walk to the pier before leaving. Randy held her hand as they walked. It seemed so natural to him. As he was getting in the car he took a last look over his shoulder, he swore he saw a paddlewheel riverboat.

Looking away he called out to Marie, "Look at that!"

Marie turned and looked, "What?" She saw nothing but the sparkling river.

"I swore I saw a riverboat, weird. It had a paddle wheel and looked old. It must be my imagination," he said, the memory of Savannah's diary came rushing back. It was real… he knew it. A message from Spirit!!

CHAPTER THIRTY-ONE

Leona and Randy

Leona needed to speak to Randy, but trying to get a free moment away from Flo lately was hard. She hovered like a mother hen, ever since she had the episode in the hospital.

They had been kept busy with planning the family reunion. Their biggest problem was finding places for them to stay. If everyone came it could be up to twenty people! Flo was sure some wouldn't be able to get the time away on short notice. They couldn't expect Blair and Boyd to close B&B Antiques in Charleston to come, even though they'd want to.

There were those that they knew would be there from Charleston: Maggie and Christian, Allison and Boyd with their baby Jasmine, Dora, Martha, Victoria, and Luke. Then there were her new friends and family members right here in New Orleans: Grace, Lenny, and his mother, Cecilia.

A smile crossed Flo's face, "Sister, why don't we ask Grace? She knows everyone."

"That's a great idea! I could use some fresh air. Why don't we give her a call and go by the office?" Leona said, having an ulterior motive.

Once she got Flo to Grace's office it was just a few miles to Randy's. She could make an excuse to stop there. Not being very proficient in texting, Leona attempted to send Randy a message, 'need your assistance coming to office have Marie distract Flo so I can talk to you'.

She looked it over, strange there was no punctuation. Did she do it right? Almost immediately a beep came through with a message from Randy. It was a picture of thumbs up. Smiling to herself, she thought that it went well. Now to get Flo out of the house.

The ladies decided to take the trolley to Mahalia's Place. It was such a beautiful day and they hadn't ridden it for some time now. It was a slow month for tourists so they had no trouble finding a seat. The clanking of the steel wheels on the tracks made a familiar sound that felt like home to Flo. The rumble under her feet and wind through the open windows were hypnotic. Her thoughts turned dark, she had tried to bury them but today they came to the surface. Talking about Leona's Wake Party was making it too real. She knew that they would meet again, this wasn't the end. But that was her brain speaking. Her heart thought differently. She silently pleaded with Ashtar, the commander of the Light Federation, for it was light we came from and light we will return to, to allow them to return together in the next incarnation.

"Come on, Flo….Flo, hello, where were you?" Leona said, yanking her arm, "It's our stop."

"Already! I must have zoned out a minute," she said, smiling.

Mahalia's Place was just a few blocks away from the trolley stop. The ladies made their way across the street and noticed how nice the neighborhood was looking. Grace's renovated homes really made a difference. She had even built new sidewalks, no more crumbling concrete and the trees along the curb added a friendly feel.

Grace was busy on the phone when the ladies walked in. She motioned for them to take a seat on the couch. Sitting there Leona noticed the beautiful painting of an older black woman. She was so drawn to it that she got up to get a closer look.

"She's calling to you, isn't she?" Grace asked.

"That's exactly how I pictured her, it's amazing! I saw her in my mind's eye, it was her," Leona said pointing to the picture.

"I found an old black and white photo of her and had my friend, Cindy, paint the portrait."

"She's happy, I feel it," Leona whispered, as in reverence.

"It was with your help that she is! I will make sure she's never forgotten," Grace got up from her chair and touched the picture frame, "Your forever in our hearts Mahalia. Now ladies, what do I owe this honor this afternoon? This seems to be my day for friends dropping by. I saw Lenny this morning."

Flo explained their unexpected visit. Although a bit macabre to some, Grace loved the idea. It fit right in with her love of all things voodoo.

And she did in fact have an answer to their visit's reason. They had just finished renovating an old three-story boarding house. Grace wanted to keep it as a hostel for young people so they kept the layout exactly like it was eighty years ago. It was equipped with a large kitchen, dining room table that sat up to sixteen, two living rooms, one that used to be used as an office, and six small bedrooms that had two single beds each.

"Grace, that would be perfect. Could we rent it for a weekend?" Leona asked.

"Absolutely not….I assume I'll be invited to this shindig sooo…it's a write-off on my taxes," she said laughing.

Leona hugged Grace and kissed her cheek, "Yes my spiritual sister, you are invited. But we must give you something."

"I've got an idea, I haven't purchased the linens for the beds yet. Will you ladies handle that?" They both nodded, "Now, what dates can I pencil you in my book on."

"We'll have to get back to you on that, we're still figuring it out. But it will be soon. I don't want to hold you up on renting the house if you need to," Flo said.

"You have just given me a great marketing idea for the house, family reunions!!" Grace said, already planning strategies in her head.

Walking back to the trolley stop, Leona suggested they pop in at Marie's office to see where she spent so much time. Flo looked at her strangely but accepted her idea. They had nothing else going on. This time Flo didn't let the rails lull her into darkness; she was already planning on a linen shopping spree at Belk.

Marie's office was on the third floor right next to Randy's. Leona wondered if Marie was going to make this move permanent; she and Randy had really hit it off.

Marie saw them coming. She wasn't sure why Granny needed Auntie Flo distracted but she'd do her best. Eventually, she'd get Leona to fess up.

"Granny, Auntie Flo, what a nice surprise!" Marie said a tad too enthusiastically.

"We were just over to see Grace and thought we'd come to see where you spend so much time," Leona said innocently.

"I was just going down to our conference room to work on my mock-up. Would you like to see it?"

"Yes, that would be nice," Flo replied, looking at Leona.

"Of course, but first, I need to use your restroom. I'll meet you there," Leona said.

Marie told her how to get to the conference room and bathroom, then linked arms with Flo and walked to the elevator. Once they were out of sight Leona ducked into Randy's office.

"Well, if it isn't Nancy Drew herself. What's with all the secrecy?" Randy said.

Leona wasted no time, "I know you read the diary, we need to talk. There are spirits at work here. I'm not sure you will understand but there's history...."

"Yes, yes there is," Randy said very calmly, "We were lovers, I know."

"You know? But how?" Leona asked dumbfounded.

"How did you know I found and read the diary?" Randy asked just as dumbfounded.

Looking at each other they burst into laughter. Once they caught their breath, Randy explained his sensitivity and family connection to Spirit. Leona told him of seeing the diary and him reading it while Marie slept. It happened during her ride in the ambulance.

"I love her, Leona. I'd like your blessing."

"That you have, son....there's just one thing. Savannah needs to complete her time here through Marie. You do realize this right?"

"More than you know. I have plans, I will make this right. For both of us!"

As they hugged Flo and Marie walked in, "Well, I hope you didn't pee in here," Flo laughed.

"Oh, hello there, no, I found the bathroom just fine," Leona replied.

"It's my fault ladies, I saw her in the hall and waylayed her into my office. She did say she was meeting you downstairs," Randy replied very innocently, looking at Leona and winking.

Now that Leona's mission was a success she tried to hurry Flo along, "Well Flo, I guess we need to let these young people get back to work."

Flo agreed and they said their goodbyes. As they walked down the hall to the elevator Marie turned to Randy and smiled, "Now that was strange, don't you think?"

"There is nothing that surprises me about your family, what we think as strange, they think as normal," Randy said laughing, as he turned to go back into his office. He knew he couldn't be around Marie much longer for fear she would start questioning him about Leona's conversation.

CHAPTER THIRTY-TWO

A Boat Trip

Grace and Lenny were waiting for Randy when he arrived at the marina. A slight breeze caused the waves to lap up over the dock every so often and the sound of the boat fenders could be heard hitting the dock. Grace had come equipped with a thermos of coffee and a bag of beignets.

"Good morning, I see you brought the essentials, Grace," Randy said following them to the boat.

"Yes, she did and I brought the rest," Lenny said, showing him a canvas bag with rope, flashlights, and tree cutters.

"I brought my compass, there's no cell service out there so GPS is useless. I learned that the hard way," Randy added, he also brought the diary which he failed to mention. He would know when the time was right to give it to Grace.

Once aboard the boat, Grace maneuvered it out into the river with ease. The cool breeze felt good against Randy's face, almost familiar. Strange, he had never been out on the river before. They traveled about fifteen minutes upriver to a tributary, checking her maps Grace announced this was the one they needed to follow. Turning the boat to the right she gingerly made her way through debris that had been floating towards the Mississippi. The waterway was a lot narrower than the river; he could imagine that at low tide many of the cypress tree roots would be exposed. Grace was right about arriving at high tide.

"We need to start looking for a dock with a cliff above it, it will be off to your right. The dock will be a mess after all these years, probably covered with black mangrove, we might need those cutters to get through," Grace announced.

She was right, the black mangroves were everywhere, along with cypress trees. They trolled for ten minutes when Lenny yelled out.

"There," he pointed, "It's there, I can see the dock. Oh my goodness, I hope there's still a path up the hill." Looking at Grace, he said, "Pull in right over there."

Pulling next to the dock wasn't as simple as it should have been. It seemed that the flow of the tributary had a strange force. It took Grace two tries before Randy's rope lashed onto the piling.

"Now that's the strangest thing, it almost felt like the water was pushing us away," Grace mumbled while helping Randy tie up the boat.

Lenny got out of the boat first, he tested the boards on the dock carefully. They seemed secure enough. Turning to the others he encouraged them to wait until he reached dry ground then come one at a time.

"You can't be too careful, this dock is very old."

After cutting back a few branches the group made their way up the hill. The growth wasn't as thick as they first thought, but the uneven ground was more worrisome.

Almost tripping on a Jasmine vine, Randy mumbled to himself, "Nope, not gonna happen this time." Lenny and

Grace looked at him strangely. "I was remembering how Marie tripped and fell, it's not going to get me, not again."

As Randy took the lead a familiar feeling came over him. It was weird, he'd not been on this path before but he knew the way. A grove of very old kumquat trees faced them as they came into a clearing, almost like they were intentionally planted there.

"Wow, in the middle of nowhere," Grace said as she searched one of the trees for fruit. "There are tiny buds, it looks like these trees are still producing, unbelievable!"

"They were, don't ask me how I know, but I do," Randy said as he continued toward where he knew the house stood.

Lenny and Grace followed looking at each other with raised eyebrows. In another few minutes, they stopped. Randy was kneeling on the ground brushing away weeds and debris from something on the ground.

Walking up behind him, Grace gasped, "Oh Lord!"

She fell to her knees and helped clean off the stone. Sitting back she looked at Randy expecting an answer, but what she saw was a strange expression on his face, a faraway look of utter sadness. Looking up to Lenny, who hadn't said a word, she cocked her head. They waited, waited for Randy to make the first move, both afraid to break the spell.

Randy looked at Grace, "There's much we need to talk about." Standing he brushed off his knees and offered a hand to help Grace up. "Let's go up to the house, I need to show you something."

The three of them continued on in silence, each in their own thoughts. Randy wondered how he was going to convince them of his story without seeming like he was delusional. Lenny's thoughts were different, upon seeing the stately old house he thought he'd seen it before, in a picture, but where? And Grace was just intrigued, she sensed Spirit was directing them.

The house was just as he had left it that morning when the helicopter landed in the clearing. Stepping up onto the porch brought all those thoughts flooding back, his heart ached for her, he had to make this right. The group made their way inside. Grace was surprised that the house still seemed structurally sound. There was still beautiful wallpaper on the walls, the humidity hadn't touched it. And some furniture was scattered about as if people had left in a hurry. She walked through the living room, stopping at the fireplace, which had been used recently.

"Did you make a fire when you were here Randy?"

"Yes, it was so dark that night and the storm made it worse. I started a fire to have light. I needed the light to read this," he took the diary out of his backpack and handed it to Grace. "You told Lenny that the house might have clues, I think this is all you need," he said sadly.

"Why didn't you just give it to me first?" Grace asked.

"Yeah, why keep it a secret?" Lenny added.

"Because, you both needed to see the house, to feel it. Grace, you know houses have souls, so does this one and the story needs to be read sitting right here," Randy said looking exhausted as if he just unburdened himself of a deep dark secret.

For the next few hours, Grace and Lenny each took turns reading the diary. Randy wandered about the grounds, touching things that brought back memories. How strange he thought, this brings me such peace. They found him standing by Savannah's tombstone. Not wanting to disturb his thoughts they waited until he noticed them. When he turned to them Grace couldn't help her enthusiasm.

"Randy, I think I can find the family from this diary! The clues are endless and the dates will be easily matched with court records. I'm sure Winnie could help us…." She added, "We need to go, now, the tide!"

They hadn't realized how long they were there. She was right, the tide would make it more hazardous walking out on the dock. The group quickly made their way back to the boat. The tide had dropped just enough to uncover rotted wood planks, thankfully their boat wasn't docked that far out. Climbing aboard Randy tossed his backpack into the boat.

"The diary Grace, where is it?" He said, panicked.

"Right here, in my pack. Not to worry, I won't let anything happen to it. It's filled with all the information we need to solve your problem," she smiled as she touched his shoulder. Grace once more maneuvered the boat out into the tributary, this time it seemed the water was intentionally pushing her away.

Before they knew it Grace was pulling the boat into the marina. Checking her watch she saw there was time to phone Winnie at the courthouse. "Well guys, I'm off to call Winnie. I'll be heading there now," she said smiling.

"Can I ride along, I came with Randy. It will save him a trip taking me back," Lenny asked.

"Sure, no problem. Randy, I'll be in touch soon," she said as they both tied the boat to the dock.

Hugging Grace, Randy said, "I can't thank you enough, I know you'll find an answer for me."

Lenny and Grace made their way to the courthouse, while Winnie was waiting for them in her office. "I'm getting ready to close up, the boss permitted me to stay for our research project. I convinced her it was the genealogy of an important resident of New Orleans," she giggled, "A little white lie."

"Actually Winnie, your little white lie might be true, let's dig in," Grace said.

It was well past eight o'clock when they realized how hungry they all were. With the information they had gathered Lenny felt like he could eat a horse.

"Ladies, my treat, let's eat!!!"

They gathered their belongings and pages of proof and made their way to the closest cafe.

"Shouldn't we phone Randy?" Winnie asked.

"Not just yet, I have one more thing to investigate," Lenny said.

"This is so unbelievable, talk about six degrees of separation!"

CHAPTER THIRTY-THREE

Lenny

Lenny couldn't wait to get home that evening. He learned in school that history repeated itself but this was crazy. Things sure had changed for him since he met Leona on that flight. Lenny had missed a real family growing up, his single mother did the best she could for him. There was never any doubt that she loved him. He couldn't imagine his life without his new family now, a real-life grandmother and sister. It was overwhelming at times but this discovery was the cherry on top.

It was late, ten o'clock. Should I take a chance? Nah, if I call this late it will scare her. He decided to call his mother in the morning when the phone rang.

Looking at the caller ID he smiled, "Hello, mom, is everything okay?"

"I don't know, why don't you tell me, Lenny," she laughed.

"As a matter of fact, I was going to call, but you already know that. I have questions that I think you can answer." Lenny replied.

They spoke for another hour, with many questions answered. Ending their conversation, they agreed to meet for brunch at ten o'clock the following morning.

Quickly texting Randy, Lenny told him to meet them the following morning adding, 'Too important to miss' and hit send. A thumbs-up came back immediately.

Morning couldn't happen fast enough for Randy, he felt that everything was coming to fruition. The cafe was crowded but he found Lenny and Cecilia sitting in a booth tucked into the rear of the cafe.

"Good morning," he said, kissing Cecilia's cheek and shaking Lenny's hand.

"Yes, it is," Lenny said as Randy sat down.

The waitress brought the third cup of coffee for Randy and the menu. The three ordered and settled into small talk until their food was delivered. Then Lenny got down to business. He caught Randy up on all the research they found last night. Handing him a picture, he waited for his reaction.

"What's this?" Randy said, then slowly his expression changed, "No way! Really?" He said looking from Lenny to Cecilia who were smiling.

"Randy, that picture is my great-great grandfather's homestead. We had no idea where it was, you see after he went to war and was killed things got crazy. The person who had that picture taken was his wife Margery. There was no record of him being married to Savannah, but his wife, Margery, referred to Savannah in her will when she died. Reed and Margery had one son, Reed II, who moved out west to find his fortune in gold. When he returned east he never reclaimed that homestead. He had indeed made a fortune and built the big house I now live in, in town." Cecilia smiled.

As if right on cue, Winnie pulled up a chair and sat down with a big beautiful smile on her face. She was enjoying the looks on their faces. Cecilia and Lenny looked at her questionably, "Well?" Lenny finally said.

"Congratulations, Cecilia," Winnie said, handing her a folder.

Cecilia opened the folder and read two very important documents. She passed the folder to Lenny who also read it.

"Is anyone going to tell me what's going on?" Randy asked exasperated.

Cecilia knew how much Randy wanted that house. Lenny had told her of the diary and his experiences. She knew how happy Lenny would be if his sister Marie ended up living there.

Thinking back to her life, Cecilia also craved a family. Being a single mother had been hard, especially being disowned once they discovered she was pregnant. Her mother refused to acknowledge her child and her father followed her blindly. The story they told the Charleston elite when they moved to New Orleans was a half-truth. Once the family attorney settled Cecilia into the family home, her parents and sister left for an extended cruise. She never heard from them again in person, only through attorneys. Her father left her enough money in a trust fund that she didn't have to work, but she did. That's how she met her husband, after Lenny was grown, who accepted her and Lenny unconditionally.

"Randy, why exactly do you want this property?" Cecilia asked

He looked at Lenny who nodded his head as if to say, it's okay. "Well, I need to make things right," he stammered.

"It's all right son, I understand more than you know, go on."

"We belong to that house, Marie and I. I have to make things right for Savannah," he said as the others noticed tears running down his cheeks, "We were supposed to raise a family there. The idea of living there, away from the riverboat business made her happy. She wanted to sit on the porch and watch our children play. Instead, I sat on the porch staring at her grave."

They knew they weren't looking into Randy's eyes, he was someone else, he was Reed. No one moved, then just as suddenly Randy was back. He stared at them, wiped the tears from his cheeks, and smiled.

"Make me an offer," Cecilia said in a whisper.

Randy's eyes opened wide. He looked at each of them, then back to Cecilia, "Do you own it?" He said, almost afraid of the answer.

"Yes, I do. Well, technically Lenny and I do. It seems we are the only survivors of my great-great grandfather's homestead. It was a terrible way to find out that my parents and sister had passed away over the years but….it is what it is. So make us an offer."

"The tax levy has been dismissed, the deed is now in their names," Winnie said, "And the best part is we are the only ones who know. You have your leverage against Amalgamated!"

"You'll sell it to me? Really, I mean for real?" Randy stammered.

"Yes," both Lenny and Cecilia said, laughing.

CHAPTER THIRTY-FOUR

Marie and Randy

Marie was just finishing up drying her hair when the doorbell rang. It had been a lazy Saturday morning and she wasn't expecting anyone. Flo and Granny had gone out an hour ago to go linen shopping for the reunion house. Opening the door she could only see a huge bouquet of yellow roses.

Laughing, she asked, "Who's behind those beautiful yellow roses, my favorite."

Dropping the bouquet just enough to see her face, Randy smiled, "I've come to kidnap you, I brought a bribe."

"Randy, you don't need to bribe me, I'd follow you anywhere," she said, pulling him into the apartment.

"I was counting on that," he said, kissing her soundly.

He explained that she needed to pack an overnight bag, nothing fancy. They were going on an adventure. Nothing like their last one, he promised, laughing. Marie didn't ask any questions, she loved surprises. Assuming it had something to do with Amalgamated, she slipped on jeans and hiking boots, threw a sweater, nightgown, and toiletries in a bag, and was ready. She left a note for Leona and Flo as they left.

Last week had been a whirlwind of activity for Randy. Taking his mother to see her investment was his first decision; she had been his biggest supporter. She loved it, but if he was planning on bringing Marie here it needed a bit of tidying up. She brought in a cleaning crew and set about making the house suitable for a weekend before the actual construction would start. Lenny had plans drawn up for him to look over but he wasn't changing anything until Marie saw the house. She still had no idea what was happening.

Randy opened the car door for Marie as she slipped into the front seat. As he walked around the car he saw two old crones peaking around the corner. Both had big smiles on their faces and were holding up the thumbs-up sign. Randy laughed and waved back. He was going to love being a part of this family.

Randy drove past the office and parked around the corner. "I just need to pick up a folder, sorry. I forgot to bring it," he said, apologizing.

"No problem, take your time. I'm all yours," Marie laughed.

Randy was back in no time, briefcase in hand. Now she knew this was more business than pleasure. Settling back in her seat she listened to the road noise, glancing over to Randy she noticed a slight smile on his face. No......it wasn't business! Sometimes she wished Spirit wasn't so giving, it would be nice to be surprised. Well, she would act surprised.

As Randy turned into the airport Marie was surprised, "Where are we going?"

"The company helicopter is here, we are going to need it today. Is that okay?"

"Yes, of course." That was all she could say.

George had the blades turning by the time they ran towards the bird. Laughing, Randy buckled her in and handed her headphones. They lifted off and cruised down the Mississippi high above the barges. Marie was in awe, the last time she was in this helicopter she was semiconscious. The views were beautiful. Randy loved watching her face, it was childlike, seeing something for the first time. George banked the bird to the right and Marie gave out a "Woah," laughing. She looked over to Randy who seemed perfectly comfortable.

Before she realized the copter was getting closer to the ground, she looked over to Randy. He was smiling, she still didn't get it. Then George turned the copter around to face the clearing. The look on her face was priceless, she really was surprised. But the surprised look disappeared and a very disappointed look took its place. Before Randy could ask her why the bird was on the ground and George was giving instructions. Marie removed her headphones and handed them to Randy. She unbuckled her belt and waited for Randy to get out first. He held out his hand and assisted her out of the helicopter, she thanked George and walked away.

Randy was dumbfounded, what went wrong? He saw happiness on her face but it faded so fast. He followed her onto the porch as the helicopter lifted off. This wasn't how he pictured it.

"Marie, what is it? You're not pleased?"

He had never seen her mad or heard her curse but for the next five minutes she berated him with what he could only imagine was the devil in her. He only heard bits and pieces before he started to put it together, so he just listened. Something about "what part of saving this house didn't you understand," to "the flow, Randy the flow," in-between, "I've worked so hard on other sites," she stopped to take a breath when he took advantage and kissed her.

"Really, really, this is your answer!" Marie said, yelling now.

He couldn't help it, he was laughing which made her all the madder. She stomped off into the house blinded by rage until she reached the living room. The fireplace had a beautiful fire blazing, a bottle of champagne was in a bucket with two glasses on the coffee table and she was speechless. Looking around the room she could see how beautiful it once was, someone had cleaned it, and the heavy dust and debris were gone.

She turned to see Randy standing in the doorway who said, "Are you calmed down a bit?"

"What's going on? Are we celebrating your company selling this property to THEM?" She said disappointedly.

"Well, you're half right, we are celebrating the sale," he said, opening his briefcase, taking out the folder, and handing it to her.

She gingerly opened the folder. She couldn't believe her eyes. It was a deed and her name was on it.

"Now that comes with one prerequisite," Randy said as he got down on one knee. "Marie, my love, will you marry me?"

"But I thought, I mean it's business and I thought, oh my Goddess!!!! Yes, yes!"

By the time she had figured it out, he had her in his arms. "This time, we'll get it right," she said, not quite understanding. But Randy did.

CHAPTER THIRTY-FIVE

Leona, Charleston

With all the preparations done, Leona and Flo sat on the veranda sipping Carolina Sweet Wine. It was good to be back in Charleston. So many things have happened in the last month. They left Grace to make the plans in New Orleans. But now it was time to get things in order here. Leona had decided to move in with her sister permanently. It just made sense, Flo would be there to care for her as her symptoms progressed. But giving up this big house had been the hardest part. Her sweet memories of her husband, Herbert, lived in each room, not to mention their son, Ronald.

"Hello ladies, permission to come aboard," yelled Dora from the courtyard.

Leona leaned over the wrought iron railing and laughed, "Welcome aboard matey!"

Hurricane Dora blew in, in her usual manner. Her striking red hair and feathered hat were the first things you saw, then came that smile and an uncomfortably long hug. They had been friends for what seemed like a lifetime. It was Dora that introduced her to the Charleston elite, the must-know people, of which Dora was one. It was over their years of friendship that they realized they both had a talent for helping Spirit. Pouring herself a glass of wine she sat down beside Leona, touching her hand.

"My dear, it seems like forever since I have seen you. Why are you back? I thought we were all doing the live wake thing in New Orleans."

"We are, but I've made a big decision that could only be addressed from here," Leona said, reaching her sister's hand. "I'm moving in with Flo permanently." She waited for Dora's reaction.

Dora accepted her decision, knowing that Leona needed to have everything in order. That was important to her. As always, she offered whatever assistance she could help with. Her heart was breaking knowing that she was losing her best friend. She vowed to help make these next months the best for Leona.

The ladies sat for the next hour reminiscing their years of hijinks. Leona laughed as Dora became more and more animated with her stories. Tears rolled down Flo's cheek from laughing so hard.

"Oh, Leona, do you remember when you and Marie got locked in the secret room in the basement?" Dora said laughing.

"That wasn't funny. Oh Lord, I thought we were done for! Thank goodness Maggie found us."

"So many wonderful memories, shall we dress up again and go to tea?" Dora asked.

"Oh, Dora, what a wonderful idea. But I'm afraid I just don't have the energy right now, rain check?"

Seeing the fatigue in Leona's eyes the ladies decided it was time for her to rest. Lifting their glasses to one last swallow Leona said, "To us, no endings, just new beginnings with Spirit."

Maggie let herself in with her key. The house was unusually quiet. Aunt Leona must be resting, she thought. Heading towards the kitchen for a cup of tea she saw Flo in the living room reading. When she got closer she realized that she had nodded off with the book in her hands. She tiptoed out of the room and made her way to the kitchen. It was hard to believe that this wouldn't be home anymore, even though she hadn't lived there in a few years, not since her marriage to Christian. But Leona had made this her home when she welcomed Maggie here as a new nurse. That seemed like so long ago now. Lost in her memories she didn't hear Flo come in.

"Child, those memories will never leave your heart," Flo whispered.

"Oh, Granny!" Maggie went into her open arms as the floodgates of tears opened up.

"I know," was all Flo could say as she stroked Maggie's back letting her cry.

They sat for a while drinking tea and remembering, that was until the doorbell rang.

Flo went to answer the door while Maggie cleaned up the teacups. Looking around the kitchen brought back so many memories. She could still see Marie standing at the window, vanquishing Abigail Calhoun's spirit and the look on everyone's face as they realized she had the gift. The gift they all had been given, the gift that brought them together.

After drying her hands with the towel, Maggie hung it on the hook, turned off the light, and headed to the living room. She hated these dismal rainy days, but they seemed to match her mood, dark.

Standing in the foyer was a gentleman, his suit and briefcase said business but his smile was friendly, more personable.

"Hello," Maggie said.

"Maggie, this is Donald McKenna. He's Leona's friend and attorney. Donald this is my granddaughter, Maggie," Flo said, introducing them.

"Very pleased to meet you, Maggie," he said with a mischievous smile.

The first thing Maggie thought was, is he flirting with me? Well, that's nonsense. He's just a nice guy, her inner voice said. It was then that Leona came down the stairs.

"Hello, Donald," she said with a huge grin.

"Miss Leona, good to see you," he said, kissing her cheek.

"You've got something for me?"

"Yes, ma'am, everything is in order. Just as you asked," he said, handing her an envelope.

Flo invited him in for coffee but he had other stops to make before heading home. He hugged Leona and nodded his respects to Flo and Maggie and was gone. Which left the three of them standing in the foyer. Neither Flo nor Maggie asked about the envelope, which made Leona feel very awkward.

"Well, I feel a bit refreshed since my nap. Why don't we see if Martha's available for dinner?" She said walking into the library.

Flo and Maggie watched her as she tucked the envelope into the top drawer of Herbert's desk. He'd been gone a long time now but she still referred to it as his.

Turning towards them she smoothed out her long flowing skirt, took a deep breath then shook out her hands. Maggie knew exactly what she was doing. It was done, she shook out the old energy and invited the new.

CHAPTER THIRTY-SIX

New Orleans

Grace was busy. Between her business, renovations, acquiring properties, and organizing Leona's reunion, she was glad Lenny had decided to come on board full time. Their relationship had started as a part-time endeavor but his expertise quickly became essential. When Grace made him the offer to be her full-time contractor, he jumped at the chance. She knew she had an edge, Winnie! It seemed Lenny was smitten and Winnie felt the same. He found his reason to stay put, no more running. Grace just cemented his commitment.

The overcast day threatened rain as Grace made her way to the office. She usually arrived first but this morning she found Lenny in the office. He was bent over a desk thumbing through blueprints.

"Morning," Lenny mumbled.

Hanging her sweater on the back of her chair, she smiled saying, "My, you're an early bird."

Looking up from the desk, he said, "Rains coming, I need to get the Randall House roof done. Coffee's brewing, should be done in a minute."

"Thanks, I need it. I was up late last night trying to assign the rooms to Leona's family and friends. She sent me a list with people she thought should room together so that gave me a head start," she said as she poured a cup of coffee. Reaching into the refrigerator she grabbed the creamer and made a mental note to pick up another container on her way home.

Lenny looked up, a sadness in his eyes, suddenly serious, "I still can't believe this. I just found my Grandmother after all these years, now I'm going to lose her."

"No, Lenny, we never lose those we love. Their soul spirit lives on in our hearts. Just as you have Jade's memories, we'll always have Leona with us. When you get sad, look at your sister, Marie. You are both here because of Leona's love for Herbert and Ronald. Our ancestors left us as their legacy," Grace said, hugging Lenny.

"Your right, Grace. It's one of those times that my heart and brain are at war," he laughed. Looking at his watch he said, "I've got to get going." He rolled up the blueprints and saluted her, "Off to the mine's, general."

Lenny understood his emotions. But honestly, he couldn't have coped so well without Winnie. She had become his rock, and their friendship quickly blossomed into romance. Winnie's concern about her family lineage didn't bother Lenny at all. In fact, he felt that she fit right in. He often teased her. What better person to understand his family connection to Spirit than a witch? Looking forward to their dinner that night made him whistle as he headed to his car.

Across town, Randy was getting ready to pitch his new site to Amalgamated. The meeting was set for ten o'clock and his boss had no idea what he was about to do. As far as he was concerned, Randy had completed the blueprints and would produce what the client contracted. Marie brought him a fresh cup of coffee and a hug for confidence.

As she turned to leave, Randy said, "Stay, you've done eighty percent of this work, you should get the credit."

"But what if they hate it," she laughed, "We'll both be out on our butts."

"They won't, I'm sure of it. And if we are, well, we'll open our own company, Winslow and Winslow!" He said as his boss came through the door.

Eyeing him strangely he said, "I hope you're not leaving us, Randy, I think you have a great future here."

"No, sir, I mean, that will depend on you," he said as he laid out the blueprints on the table. His boss busied himself on his cellphone until the clients from Amalgamated showed up. With all the introductions made, Randy made his pitch.

"Gentleman, we had two concerns on the property. The first one is the access roads that need to be built. When we pulled preliminary permits it alerted environmental groups. It seems that the acres bordering the northern property are protected, so we might have a problem." He looked around to see raised eyebrows. He continued, "The second is the pier. The price to build the size that would facilitate your plant would be astronomical. The area would have to be dredged and that would change the flow of the tributary temporarily. But we feel that the tributary is too small for the ships you'd like to bring in," he paused.

And when he did, a barrage of questions started. The look on his boss's face was telling. If he didn't convince these guys to love the new site he was toast. He looked over to Marie and smiled, this was her cue.

"Please, we have a solution," she said in the sweetest little girl voice. They couldn't help but listen. "Gentleman, the site I'm about to show you will solve all your problems and save you millions," she had their attention. Two gentlemen sat forward in their seats wanting to hear more. "The new site we're proposing already has access from major highways and the river! A more than adequate pier needing minimal upgrades will service your plant directly from the Mississippi. The existing plant appears to be structurally sound. Of course, you'd have to outfit it to fit your specs, but you're not building from scratch. All of which will save you millions, as I said before," she held her breath.

The gentlemen stood and Marie's heart sank, they had lost. She looked over to Randy who was smiling. Marie gave him a look and he cocked his head towards the men. She turned to see them all bending over the table looking at the blueprints, mumbling to each other. Randy thought he heard one of them say this was by far a better site. The worst part was his boss, Mr. Holmes, giving them a thumbs-up sign with a scowl on his face.

Amalgamated signed a contract for the new site. It was a few hours later after the clients left that Mr. Holmes expressed his displeasure to them both.

"You do realize that you could have cost this firm millions of dollars? We had this conversation three weeks ago, Randy, when I distinctly told you to draw up plans on the original site."

Fearlessly, Marie said, "Sir, it was me. I drew up the backup site. Randy had nothing to do with it. I found it and convinced him to let me try. He was just trying to allow me to show you what I was capable of. He did the plans for the original site as you requested." Once again she found herself holding her breath.

"You've got spunk, girl. I'll say that for you," he paused as both Randy and Marie waited for their walking papers. "I have another client that I think you both could help. She is very environmentally connected. Your penance will be to please her, and believe me, she's not a pushover like me," he said smiling. "Check with Betty, my secretary, she has the contracts. Randy, Marie, good job," he said, shaking both their hands as he then walked out laughing.

"What was that all about, oh my Goddess, I thought we were done for," Marie said.

"Jeez, I was already planning our new logo for our company in my head," Randy replied.

It suddenly dawned on them, they weren't fired. As they laughed and hugged, Marie suggested they get their new assignment before he changed his mind. Walking hand and hand down the hall they nearly bumped into Mrs. Holmes.

"Good morning, ma'am, nice to see you," Randy sputtered.

"Just the people I was looking for," she said, as she tossed her thousand-dollar handbag over her shoulder, "When do we begin?"

"Ma'am? Begin what?" Randy asked.

"My new conservatory, of course. My husband said you both are the best. And I only hire the best," Mrs. Holmes said.

Randy and Marie looked at each other, they wanted to laugh but didn't. This was their penance. They understood now why Mr. Holmes was laughing as he left.

With the Amalgamated project well on its way, Randy felt like he could breathe for the first time in weeks. His goal now was to get Marie back out to the homestead, show her the plans, and start renovations. But he had just a few more details to finalize. Pulling out his cellphone he punched in Grace's number.

"Good morning, Mahalia's Place. Grace speaking," she said, not recognizing the number.

"Morning, Grace, it's Randy. I hope I didn't catch you at a bad time."

She assured him that she wasn't busy at the moment. He had a proposal that he was sure she'd jump on board with, crossing his fingers he dove in.

"As you know, Lenny drew up plans for the renovation of the homestead. I'd like him to be the lead contractor on the job. Now I understand he's your employee and I don't want to step on any toes but here's what I'm proposing," Randy filled Grace in on his plan as she listened.

"I love it! Yes, please go ahead with your plan. I will make sure that Lenny is free from any obligations here. He will be overwhelmed at first, he's very dedicated, but once we get him on board it will be fine," Grace said enthusiastically.

Feeling like the weight of the world had lifted just a bit, Randy tackled his next step, Marie. Using the excuse of needing aerial photos for their project, Randy invited Marie along for the ride. As they drove out to the airfield Marie talked endlessly about their project and the ideas she was incorporating. Her enthusiasm increased as she spoke of her meeting with Mr. Holmes, who had offered her a full-time position. Of course, she suspected Randy had something to do with that. He quickly denied that allegation and informed her that it was the Amalgamated team that had insisted on her being brought on full-time.

Once again, George had the copter blades ready to go. Running with heads bent down they made their way inside. Headphones and seatbelts on, Randy gave George the thumbs up and they were off. Almost immediately Marie noticed they were headed upstream not down. Randy was watching out the window smiling as she tapped him on the shoulder. Turning he could see she was confused. He just smiled and pointed to his headphones and shrugged his shoulders. She thought his headphones weren't working. It was too loud to ask without them, so she just settled back to enjoy the ride.

When George banked right above the tributary she knew, they were headed to the homestead. What a wonderful surprise she thought as she looked down at her engagement ring. One day we'll be able to drive home instead of using a helicopter.

George landed the copter with ease in the clearing, Randy jumped out and helped Marie down. He held up two fingers to George who nodded and lifted the copter back in the air.

Marie stood for the first time, really taking it all in. She walked out to the bluff, as Randy watched. It was so overgrown you could hardly see the river. There were cypress, black mangroves, and thousands of wild crepe myrtles. Marie made a mental note, this was her priority. Turning she saw Randy sitting on the steps of the house smiling. As she started forward something caught her eye, it was the stone. The stone she had tripped over and hit her head. She knelt to the ground and started clearing off the debris reverently. Marie knew it was Savannah's stone, she had to make it right. Wiping away the last of the weeds and grass, she could see it. Beautifully engraved under her name was, "Another lifetime, another love. I will find you."

She hadn't realized that Randy was kneeling beside her as the tears rolled down her cheeks. He wiped away the tears and hugged her. As they cleared away grass from around the stone, Marie thought it would make a beautiful centerpiece for a flower garden. She decided this would be her first priority, the bluff second.

Silently, they stood and brushed the leaves off their pants. Marie was the first to break the spell.

"A rose garden, yes, yellow roses. We'll start here," she pointed as Randy listened. "It will be dedicated to her, Savannah's Garden," she said, finally looking at him, smiling. Taking her hand Randy led her onto the porch.

"We have two hours before George comes back. I have a few things to discuss with you about the house."

"Okay, lead the way, sir," Marie replied.

They stepped into the foyer where a big round table was covered with blueprints. Marie went over and started looking at them. He could see the wheels turning in her head.

"Marie, you have the final say on everything," he said gently, not to overwhelm her.

"Randy, are these the original plans?"

"Actually, no, these are the plans Lenny drew up. Would you like to see what he thinks the original looked like?"

"Yes, please."

Randy flipped over two pages to reveal a very different floor plan. Marie looked at it closely.

"Well there's no way we can go back to 1855, that's for sure!" She said laughing. "There's no kitchen, and look, they added these walls to make the foyer. I wonder which generation did this. I thought no one lived here for over a hundred years?"

"Lenny and Winnie did a deep dive into any permits that might have been issued to this homestead. In 1920 they found that a family member started renovating but suddenly stopped, never completing the work," Randy said.

"Well, I like it just the way it is now. A bit of paint and maybe a second bedroom would be nice," she smiled.

Leading her away from the foyer into the living room, he sat down on the old sofa and motioned her to sit next to him. "Marie, your brother, and his mother sold this place to us. You do know that right?"

"Yes, I've thanked them a hundred times. Lenny's threatened to beat my butt if I mentioned it again," she said laughing, "Why?"

"I want Lenny to be the lead contractor on the renovation. Grace has cleared the way, but there's one other thing. I'd like for us to designate this homestead in the historical registry if it qualifies. Grace could spearhead the details and I'd like it to be known as The Renard House or Homestead. Whichever you choose, if you agree," he said, looking at her questionably.

"Randy, that's a great idea! In honor of Savannah and Reed! I love it!" She hugged him and then stood up. "We've got to find pictures, there must be some. Pictures of them to hang on the wall, right there in the foyer." After calming down a bit, she said, "Homestead, I like The Renard Homestead. But I must ask Lenny before we make a final decision," she said, plopping back down on the couch, exhausted at all the ideas rolling around in her head. I'll make this a home, Savannah, I promise, one with children playing in the yard as Randy and I grow old together.

CHAPTER THIRTY-SEVEN

The Family Gathers

The gathering had begun. As Grace, Leona and Flo fluffed pillows and smoothed bedspreads upstairs, Marie and Winnie were in the kitchen preparing hor'dourves for later. Happy laughter filled the house. One would not believe they were preparing for a wake.

"Anyone home?" Maggie giggled loudly as she came through the door.

Marie was the first to react, running into the living room to embrace Maggie and Christian.

"Hi guys, it seems like forever!" Noticing Winnie standing behind her she quickly introduced them all.

As Maggie hugged her, she said, "So, this is the woman who captured my cousin's heart. Welcome to this crazy family."

"You have no idea how well she fits in," Marie laughed. "How was the drive? Long I presume."

"Yes, it was. We decided to make it more than just a weekend. I want to enjoy my hometown like a tourist," Maggie laughed.

Leona, Grace, and Flo made their way downstairs hearing the commotion. Flo watched her sister, all this laughter is good medicine. Before they could finish hugging everyone, Dora and Martha arrived. Dora wore her signature feathered hat to match her outfit. Martha was carrying Carolina Sweet Wine, complaining that the airlines would only allow her to bring two bottles. It was a joy to see the family coming together.

After all the pleasantries were exchanged, Grace suggested, "Why don't I show y'all to your rooms to freshen up? Then you can join us in the parlor for refreshments."

"Lead the way, Miss Grace. Dora, may I take your bags for you?" Christian offered.

"Why thank you, kind sir," Dora said, in the longest drawn-out southern drawl she could muster. Which led to another round of laughter.

Thirty minutes later the group was reassembled back downstairs. Marie and Winnie had the dining room table covered with all kinds of finger food. Today, Friday's fare would be light, tomorrow's a bit more formal. As they sat and chatted, Maggie got to know Winnie better and Christian ambled through the house checking out the renovations.

Lenny found him on the back porch, "You're a sight for sore eyes. I was feeling outnumbered."

The two shook hands. "I know how you feel. How are you doing? I hear you're no longer traveling," Christian asked.

"No more rambling for me," Lenny laughed, "Grace made me an offer I couldn't refuse. Then, of course, there's Winnie."

"Yes, we've met. Marie said she fits right in."

"She's been a big help to Randy and me, working at the courthouse," he mumbled.

Sensing he wanted to change the subject, Christian said, "These renovations look great. Did you have the original plans?"

Lenny was more than willing to talk about construction. He explained the history of the house as they walked through and Grace's idea to keep it as a hostel for young people to enjoy the city on a budget. Christian loved the idea of what Grace was doing in New Orleans; he wondered if it could be done in Charleston. There were some areas in dire need of rehabilitation there also. It might be something he could discuss with Boyd in the future.

The next to arrive were Victoria and Luke, the youngest of the new family. Being newly married they still considered themselves honeymooners and acted like it. They drove from Savannah after a visit with Luke's parents.

As Victoria hugged Leona, she said, "Thank you for including us this weekend. I've missed you."

"You're very welcome my dear. I hope you and Luke will continue to be part of our very extended family for a long time," Leona said laughing.

As everyone was getting caught up with the latest news Leona watched and listened. The room seemed to get louder with laughter and she sensed the house liked this. She smiled thinking about the legacy she would be leaving and wondering who she would meet up with in her next incarnation. They were all connected in one way or another in past lives, that's what brought them together now. The best part was that they were all aware. It made saying goodbye a little easier.

It was close to sundown when Allison, Boyd, Blair, and Brooks got there. Once again a rowdy welcome ensued.

"We're so sorry we are late. Unfortunately, we experienced a flat tire along the way," Boyd blurted out.

"No problem, we're all here now," Leona said looking at Allison, "Except for our latest addition. Where is Jasmine Grace?"

"Well, that's another story. She's teething and very cranky lately. So Luke's mom, Grace, volunteered to come to stay with her in Charleston," Allison gave a nod to Luke, smiling. "She is, after all, another grandmother. My daughter is blessed with so many!"

"And," Luke butted in, "Both my parents send their love. They would have come but business took my Da back to Scotland. And, as for Marm, well, Allison needed her," he said with affection.

Marie suddenly noticed the time, where was Randy? He should have been here by now. Checking her cell phone for messages she realized her battery had run down. Quickly turning to Maggie she asked to borrow her phone. He didn't answer her call, maybe he didn't recognize Maggie's number. She looked up to see Lenny headed her way.

"Marie, where's your phone? Randy has been trying to get a hold of you."

"My battery died, I guess I forgot to plug it in last night. I tried to call him on Maggie's phone but he didn't pick up. What's up? Where is he?" she asked.

"He said he was running an errand for Leona and got waylaid. Evidently it took longer than he expected. But he's on his way now," Lenny explained.

It was a wonderful afternoon. The blended family talked, laughed, and cried recalling their memories of coming together. Someone mentioned Mr. Calhoun and an enormous cheer went up. It was appropriate that he be here. After all, he brought many of them together. Maggie suggested that he be inducted into their family officially. Dora called for a vote and the resounding sound of ayes could be heard above the laughter.

"Was that roar of approval for my entrance?" Randy asked as he walked into the parlor.

"For those of you that don't know him, this is my fiancé," Marie said, proudly walking over and linking arms with him. "Everyone, this is Randy."

"Sorry I'm late, my meeting ran longer than expected," he said, turning his head ever so slightly and winking at Leona. She responded with a nod.

As daylight progressed to nighttime the party started to wind down. Those that had traveled were excusing themselves for some much-needed sleep. Flo and Dora could see Leona nodding off in her chair. Without bringing attention to her directly, Flo announced that she was getting tired. Gathering around the two women they all gave Leona and Flo their hugs and love. Tomorrow promises to be a busy day.

CHAPTER THIRTY-EIGHT

Good-bye and Surprises

The morning was coming way too fast as Marie made her way home. She and Randy had stayed up with some of the others playing cards and reminiscing. When she got back to the condo she checked on her grandmother who was sleeping soundly. After thanking the Spirits she snuggled into her bed. It had been a wonderful day, one she will always treasure. As she drifted into the twilight stage of sleep she heard, ***"Thank you, dear sister."*** Marie slept soundly and deeply with no further interruption.

Leona woke with a start, this was the day she'd waited and planned for. She felt energy she hadn't had in a while. These next two days were going to reveal big surprises. She hoped Lenny and Randy had completed their portion; she had done hers with Winnie and Donald, her attorney, back in Charleston's help.

The group at Grace's hostel was starting to gather in the kitchen. Each in search of coffee and beignets. Dora and Martha were already up and setting out the pastries.

"I'm going to miss our dear Leona," Martha said absently as she set out coffee mugs.

"We all will, dear sister. But this is not the time for sorrow, this is a celebration of life." Dora replied, hugging her.

Maggie came into the kitchen and watched the two women she admired so much thanks to Leona. "Okay ladies, we'll have enough time for tears later. Let's show Leona our love and support now."

Upon seeing Maggie, the two older women broke out crying. "Oh, Maggie." They both hugged her tightly, "You are such a big part of Leona's legacy. Please don't forget us!"

"Forget you? Ladies, you are my family! Let's pull it together……..Leona will be here soon. It's time for us to love and laugh with each other. She may be leaving us in body but never spirit….she will live on within all of us," Maggie said with a single tear rolling down her cheek.

As the rest of the group was mingling in the living room drinking coffee and catching up with each other there was a knock at the door. Allison, being the closest, answered the knock. A young man stood with an envelope, "Madam….this is for your family." He handed it to her and walked away.

Allison turned, looking at the group puzzled. "What is it, honey?" Boyd asked.

"It's for us….a letter?" Allison said.

"Well, open it my dear" Dora said.

Allison tore open the end and pulled out an invitation, she read it out loud.

My dear family, you are cordially invited to a surprise afternoon.

Please dress casually and bring your appetite. Your driver will arrive at noon to whisk you all away. Love, Leona

The room erupted in a hundred questions, each looking at each other for answers. There were no answers. As the questions simmered to a dull roar they agreed that Leona had planned her wake well, they were surprised.

The day was perfect, sunny with a hint of a cool breeze and not a cloud in the sky. Leona had planned on a limo to pick up those who lived in New Orleans and weren't staying at Grace's that afternoon. They were to meet the rest of the family at a celebration spot only a few knew the destination.

Randy had arranged for Marie to ride with him. They had one last thing to do before the celebration. The final contracts had come in for Amalgamated and his boss wanted them signed off asap. Although Marie was anxious to visit with the family she regretfully agreed to the meeting.

Flo realized that Leona needed to take things slow, so they lingered over coffee and talked about how wonderful it was to see the others. Flo got the feeling that there was more to Leona's lingering than the need for energy. She seemed more alive today than in the past weeks, which pleased and worried Flo. Was this her last hurrah?

The morning passed quickly as everyone prepared for their outing. They began gathering around eleven thirty in the living room, talking excitedly about what was to come. Promptly at noon, they heard the clanking of a loud trolley bell outside Grace's hostel. Looking out the window Martha giggled.

"It's our ride y'all! A bus that looks like a trolly!

"Only Leona would send a traditional New Orleans ride, let's go, guys! I can't wait to see what's next," Christian yelled, pointing them all out the door.

The ride took them outside the city, as the cement faded into magnolias and cypress the conversations dwindled.

"I never realized how beautiful it was this far out!" Dora said.

"I can't imagine where she's taking us, a picnic maybe? At an old plantation?" Victoria wondered out loud.

"Wherever it is, it will be awesome......I just know it," Martha replied.

At the same time Leona's limo arrived at the condo, Geraldine, Lenny, and Winnie were already inside when Flo and Leona got in. After making herself comfortable she looked at them and smiled, a very mischievous smile. Lenny gave a slight nod of his head as she winked at him. All was well in her world.

Marie and Randy were on their way to the office when his cell phone rang. Looking over to Marie he said, "It's the boss." Marie listened to the one-way conversation, hearing too many "Yes Sir" and "Right away sir."

When he finally hung up Marie asked, "What was that all about?"

Looking upset he replied, "I'm sorry honey, we have one stop before going to the office. It seems Mrs. Holmes has a change in her plans for the conservatory she needs us to look at."

"Today? Oh Randy, my family," she whispered sadly.

His heart broke for her, "We'll do this quickly I promise, then we'll sign the papers with Amalgamated and I'll turn my phone off for the rest of the weekend. Deal?"

Marie nodded absently looking out the window. All she could think about was her Granny.

Randy gently took her hand and squeezed it.

The trolley slowed to a crawl and pulled off on a dirt road. Looking around they could see fresh debris off to the side.

"This road has just been cut, it looks like a bulldozer came through here!" Boyd stated.

"Wow, where the heck are we going?" Was said by three or four of them.

As they crawled along the road Martha noticed a clearing up ahead, "Look y'all! Oh my goodness there's a house in those woods!"

As if in unison they all stood up to look…sure enough there was an old house. The closer they got they noticed the beautiful yellow roses that lined the front porch in large vases along with several rocking chairs.

"How quaint, I wonder if this is Leona's house?" Allison asked.

"If it is she never told me about it, maybe it's Flos," Dora replied.

The trolley pulled up to the makeshift walkway still covered in weeds. The driver opened the doors and announced this was the last stop. As they exited the trolley a woman came out the front door dressed as if she was going to a ball in the eighteen hundreds. Her yellow ball gown matched the roses beautifully.

"Welcome to the Renard Homestead," she said smiling, "My name is Cecilia Renard, would you please join me inside? We have much to talk about."

Taken aback the group silently followed her into the house, each thinking this was not at all what they expected!

As the trolley made its way back down the dirt road it pulled over so Leona's limo could pass by.

"What a strange place for a trolley bus….actually, this is a strange place for us also! What are you up to dear sister?" Flo asked, smiling.

As they pulled up to the house in the clearing, Geraldine asked, "Is this the house Marie had her accident at? Auntie, what do you have up your sleeve?"

Leona just smiled and pointed. Cecilia stood proudly on the porch once again beckoning them to come in.

"Oh jeez, she really took this seriously," Lenny whispered to Leona.

"Well, she was the rightful heir. I thought it was just the right touch."

As the family was gathering at the Renard Homestead, Marie and Randy had just finished up business at the Holmes house and were headed to the office.

"I really don't understand why this couldn't have waited till Monday. Moving one-half of the wall in the blueprints was no big deal," Marie complained.

"Well, Mr. Holmes did warn us she was demanding."

"Yes, I get it. Our penance for disobeying him..... whatever."

Randy could tell she was getting more aggravated by the minute. "I'll drive faster, we'll run in and out and be on our way, I promise." He said looking at her as if defeated.

"Oh Randy, I'm sorry. It's not your fault. I'm being a brat, I just wanted today to be perfect for Leona," she said with a half smile, "Do you forgive me?"

Feeling all the more guilty he just nodded. As they pulled up to the office his cell phone beeped a text message, 'ready when you are.' Marie idly looked at the phone sitting on the console and read it to Randy. Never noticing who sent it she said, "Great they're ready, let's get this done!"

Randy's secretary had all the paperwork set out on the table, "Amalgamated signed there's this morning, they had a board meeting to get to. Yours are here, just sign each page where the sticky tag is," she said winking at Randy.

Seeing the stack of papers Marie started signing, one after the other never really reading any of them. Then she looked up and passed them to Randy. Smiling he did the same. As he thanked his secretary, Marie was halfway out the door and didn't notice the paper he slipped into his jacket pocket.

As they got into the car he took a deep breath. He hadn't planned this part. How was he going to explain leaving the city when she was expecting to go to Grace's? Putting his hands on the wheel he turned to Marie and asked, "Do you trust me?"

"Yes, of course, I do. What's wrong?" She said concerned.

"We have one more stop," he said holding his breath and closing his eyes, waiting for the eruption. But there was silence, peeking out of one eye he saw she was smiling. "Are you okay?" He said timidly, not understanding her reaction.

"Randy, take me wherever you want. I have faith in you." She said genuinely, smiling.

He bent over and cupped her face as he kissed her knowing this was their destiny. "Your future awaits my lady." He said as they drove off.

It wasn't long before Marie realized they were headed out of town, in the direction of their new house. She sat silently waiting. When Randy turned onto a newly made dirt road she remarked astonished, "Randy, when did you do this? The last time we came here it was nothing but a thick brush?"

"Lenny's crew did it last week. They needed an access road to start the renovations."

"So, you're here to check on the progress?" She asked.

"Something like that."

When they pulled up to the house Marie saw the yellow roses first, then she saw Cecilia.

"Randy, what's going on? Are we celebrating Leona here?"

"Something like that."

Randy and Marie walked up to the porch as Cecilia greeted them, "Welcome home!" She kissed them both on the cheek, "Come in, we're all here."

The first thing Marie saw was Leona smiling so brightly it was almost like a ray of light shot out of her. Not quite understanding, Marie ran to hug Leona. "What a grand idea celebrating here Granny," looking around she saw everyone mingling about, "and everyone's here, was this your idea?"

"Something like that," she said with a wink.

Before she could question her Cecilia gently touched her elbow and whispered in her ear, "I'll need a moment of your time my dear. Please come with me."

Marie looked at Leona who just smiled and nodded. Cecilia took her hand as they walked to the back of the house. She told Marie the family story once again as she opened the bedroom door. Maggie stood smiling, "Your lifetimes are about to be connected," she said.

"Maggie! What is this?"

Maggie turned and opened the closet doors, and hanging there was the most beautiful emerald green ball gown. Suddenly Marie heard, ***"Wear it for me, for us"*** and she knew who's dress it was.

"How? Where?" She could only sputter, looking from Maggie to Cecilia.

"Old family trunks, lots of research," Cecilia said smiling.

"But why? Why today? Why this weekend? This is Leona's time."

A soft knock at the door answered her questions, it was Leona. "I'm sure by now you are completely confused, my dear. Sit while I explain," Marie sat on the edge of the bed as Leona explained, "My time is short, as you are aware. I wanted to experience all the joys I could while I'm still here. Knowing that you and Randy were engaged I asked him if he wouldn't mind engaging in some shenanigans. The emerald green ball gown was Savannah's, she never got to go to the ball. Spirit told me it was to be your wedding gown," she paused to let Marie catch up, "I'd like to be at my only granddaughter's wedding before I go."

"Granny, that's a beautiful idea, but how? I mean what about a preacher?"

"I'm an ordained minister, my dear," Cecilia smiled.

"There's also the license, I mean city hall…?" She asked.

"Remember all those papers you signed this morning? Winnie got the license and gave it to Randy's secretary. You signed it this morning," she said holding the paper that Randy had slipped into his jacket pocket a few hours ago.

Suddenly Marie burst into laughter, it was so joyish that the other ladies joined in. By the time they settled down tears were rolling down their cheeks. "Okay ladies, I'm in your hands, let's do this!"

Meanwhile, the stage was being set. A beautiful yellow rose archway was set up near Savannah's stone with vases of roses surrounding it as the family gathered.

"I'm not sure how you managed this Randy but I give you a lot of credit! I know Marie was probably ready to explode by the time you got to the office," Lenny asked.

"It was definitely a lesson in patience for me. But we did it!" He said, slapping Lenny's back, "Thank you for the road, it was a genius idea!"

"You were going to need it eventually," he said smiling.

There was a sudden hush in the crowd as the front doors opened and Cecilia walked out, "Places everyone, it's time!" She said as she walked to the front of the archway. As if on cue there was music, soft and soulful.

Randy watched as Marie walked out of the house onto the porch. Suddenly he wasn't himself, he felt Reed and saw Savannah in that split second. He knew without a doubt they would make it this time. His face lit up and he smiled as the love he had waited a lifetime for walked toward him.

The celebration lasted till early evening, banquet food had been catered and servers were there to assist with any request. The music was low enough to enjoy a conversation but loud enough to dance to. Leona sat back and watched the next generation take their rightful place. She knew her legacy was through them, as hers was from her ancestors.

The trolley and limousine showed up promptly at eight o'clock as planned by Leona. The family going back to Graces piled onto the trolley, tired but happy. Leona kissed Randy and her granddaughter good night before heading to the limo. She'd see them all tomorrow for her final surprise.

Sunday morning the rain came, it was almost as if the heavens were crying. There were no early risers today, most had stayed up way too late talking spnd enjoying each other's company.

Leona decided to have breakfast with the rest of the family as did Flo. They headed over to Graces where they found a few already in the kitchen cooking bacon and sausage.

"Good morning all, that smells good. I didn't realize I was hungry until just now," Leona said sitting down at the table as Dora handed her a cup of coffee.

"Good morning to you too. You're looking pretty chipper for this miserable day," Dora said.

"Miserable, never. It's just the heavens replenishing Mother Earth's lifeblood. It's water dear sister, what we share with her, the ebb and flow of life," Leona said almost reverently.

Dora knew Leona wasn't just speaking of the rain as she gazed at her longtime friend. She could see the ebb and flow of Leona's life fading. She vowed that very minute to make each moment a joyful one. And as if on cue, a ray of sunlight came through the window and the rain stopped. Dora looked over to Leona and winked, they smiled at each other knowing what only long-time friends understood.

Breakfast turned into brunch as people wandered down or in during the morning. The casualness of family enjoying each other had settled into a relaxed atmosphere. Christian was seen napping on the hammock out back while Boyd cleaned the grill for dinner later. Cecilia and Allison were deep into a conversation about some charity while Maggie and Allison were giggling like school girls about something amusing to them only. When Marie and Randy showed up the noise level rose a few octaves. After everyone settled back down Leona signaled Dora.

"Can I have your attention please, Leona has a few words to say?"

The family gathered around finding seats where they could. Boyd dragged out a few dining room chairs for others.

"First let me say it's been an honor to be here this weekend. Not many people get to attend their own wake. But you know me, I do things differently, sometimes it works and sometimes it doesn't. But either way, there are lessons to be learned. This weekend I learned what a loving and giving family I have. You all showed such grace by allowing this to happen," she paused looking at each one, stopping at Marie, "Especially my granddaughter who allowed me to commandeer her wedding day," Marie blew her a kiss as a tear trickled down her cheek, "I am forever grateful that you all helped in that endeavor and we were able to celebrate it. My only regret is that Ronald and Fatu couldn't see their beautiful daughter so happy." Suddenly exhausted, she sat down, and Dora and Maggie rushed to her side.

"Leona, you need to rest, we can finish this later," Dora pleaded.

Maggie handed her a glass of water, the room was so still Leona had to laugh, "I'm not dying yet, just tired, relax everyone," she said smiling. You could hear a collective breath being taken as they whispered among themselves.

"I need to finish this up so we can all enjoy the rest of the day. Maggie, please stay here with me," she said reaching for her hand. Dora walked to the table and brought back an envelope she handed to Leona. "I need to finalize a few things today, so here goes," she took a gulp of water and waved Christian over to sit beside her. "To my first born grandchild, Marie, I have set up a trust fund for you and your children, of which there will be many. I have also made arrangements to pay off the mortgage on your wonderful homestead." She said, smiling at Marie and Randy, "Lenny, my second grandchild, I give you a large yearly allotment. Use it wisely, make it work for you." She said smiling at him, "Now that I know they are taken care of and I will be living in New Orleans I decided that my next heir, my grandniece, Maggie, will inherit Harrington House and its belongings," Leona handed Maggie the envelope, "This is the deed to the house, it's already in your name my dear."

"But Aunt Leona, what about your sister, my grandmother?" Maggie questioned.

"Our time is dwindling, I want Harrington House to thrive, be alive again. It needs young blood. You and Christian have made Charleston your home, now please make Harrington House your forever home. I am confident that as long as you live there it will remain a gathering place for our family, young and old."

"Auntie, you're not the only one with a surprise," she glanced over to Christian who nodded and smiled, "Harrington House will be filled with laughter and love, I promise! We're pregnant!"

The room erupted into laughter and tears. There wasn't a dry eye in the group, everyone stood to embrace Leona and Maggie. They had been the glue that brought them all together and created a bond for life.

Leona sat back and took mental snapshots, she wanted to remember this forever, engraving it in her memory for the next time they would meet. She did not doubt that her family had been here before in some strange capacity or another. Where will Spirit have us gather in the next lifetime? she wondered.